CROSSED PATHS

Also written by Bill Schneider:

Second Chapter (iUniverse)—2005

Sand Dollar (iUniverse)—2006

www.BillSchneider.us

CROSSED PATHS

A Novel

Bill Schneider

ASJA Press
New York Lincoln Shanghai

Crossed Paths

ASJA Press
an imprint of iUniverse, Inc.

iUniverse books may be ordered through booksellers or by contacting:

iUniverse
2021 Pine Lake Road, Suite 100
Lincoln, NE 68512
www.iuniverse.com
1-800-Authors (1-800-288-4677)

This is a work of fiction. All of the characters, names, incidents, organizations, and dialogue in this novel are either the products of the author's imagination or are used fictitiously.

ISBN-13: 978-0-595-42748-2
ISBN-10: 0-595-42748-0

Printed in the United States of America

In memory of A. Alan Crosby, who left us far too soon …
but touched the hearts of many.

We have old friends
Some are memories
Who come and tap us on the shoulder
Then they take us to the places that we miss
And remember with a smile …
We go where there is love
And then it holds us closely
By going back in time
We find enough love stayed behind
To make us feel we are home
—Jane Olivor

CHAPTER 1

Tomorrow morning I depart on a book-signing tour to promote my recent novel. The first stop on the junket is Nashville, Tennessee, which seems odd to me because I'm not a huge fan of country music.

Most anyone else would be thrilled to go on a ten-day, five-city tour to peddle flesh. That's what we writers refer to as press junkets. My father referred to these road trips as dog and pony shows. But I'm not like most anyone. At least that's what Alex, my literary agent keeps telling me.

While packing for my trip, Alex calls to remind me about the promotional opportunities he's working on for the annual tourism conference in Nashville. The prospect of a simple book signing dissipates while I listen to my agent's exuberance.

"Will, think about the possibilities."

"I'm thinking."

"Three thousand tourism industry professionals in the same hotel as you … oh Will, it's just too much to imagine."

"Wow. I'm thinking of winning a free ticket to some exotic destination. Am I headed in the right direction?"

"Please, don't take a tone with me."

"What tone? I'm trying to get excited."

"It's the possibility of magic that should excite you, Will."

I toss a basketball in the air. "Possibilities don't excite me, Alex. Reality does."

"Matt Damon is much more low maintenance."

"Matt Damon is going to be in Nashville?"

"No."

"Then maybe you should have him make an appearance."

"Funny, Will. Anyone else would jump at the chance to mingle with all of these travel folks. It all comes down to one thing: selling your book. And Will…. no one can do it better in person than you. Your charm and charisma turn heads."

"Alex, I'm happy to hear I'm not like anyone else."

"You are so lucky to be going to Nashville," he said in his usual upbeat and encouraging way. Of course, if I was really lucky, I would be staying home working on my next novel instead of heading to Nashville. While the compliments he bestowed on me were enticing, Alex had given this lecture to me many times before … so many times that I was close to having it memorized. Despite his perseverance, Alex failed to convince me the first stop in Nashville was vitally important to my career. The annual tourism convention was held in San Francisco last year, which I would have much preferred attending, since it's only an hour away by plane and I have lots of friends there. San Francisco would have been more manageable. Plus there's no time change between Los Angeles and San Francisco. Instead, what am I doing? I'm schlepping to Nashville.

Trust me … after doing more book signings than I would care to remember, it all comes down to pressing the flesh. While that may sound insincere, please let me explain. Writers, by nature, are an insecure lot. Most of us would rather stay at home and work on our next project than go out and promote our last writing. We're just born that way.

And in this day and age of active litigation, I tend to be cautious when making broad generalizations. However, I will go on record saying to any writer who vehemently disagrees with my proclamation that writers generally prefer not to self promote, if I am really off the mark, please let me know when you want to fill in for me at my next book signing.

Having made that proclamation, let me also pontificate my belief that publicists and agents are supreme flesh peddlers. They live and breathe ways to help promote a writer. Most everyone will defend the hard work of agents and publicists as doing what is required to help promote their clients. But as a writer, I view their efforts as somewhat contradictory. That is to say they may have my best interests at heart when it comes to the economics of bookselling, but when one thinks about the mental well being of a writer, publicists and agents are really a writer's biggest nemesis. My therapist would advocate they erect a barrier around a writer's mental health, and for that sound piece of advice, she would charge you handsomely by the hour.

Welcome to my world. Having unintentionally bored you with the travails of a writer's dichotomy, I will simply say I am procrastinating, which is the art of a writer at a loss for words.

I glanced through the conference schedule while the flight was boarding. As people passed by me and intermittently bumped my arm, aimed their carry-on bags toward my leg or brushed against my seat, I realized just how narrow airplane aisles had become. But then I remembered I don't have to do this for a living, and ordinarily I would only have a ninety-second commute from my living room to the study. That thought brought a smile to my face.

"Hello."

I looked up to find a woman with jet-black hair, piled above her head, secured by an enamel chop stick, wearing a long flowery skirt and a silk blouse underneath a cashmere sweater. "Is this your seat?" she asked.

"Yes."

As she struggled to put her bag in the overhead bin, I instinctively stood up to help her.

"Thanks, but I can do this. My husband told me I have to fend for myself."

Her perfume was subtle. I exhaled a sigh of relief as I anticipated a quiet flight, relieved that I shouldn't have to answer a lot of questions for the next few hours. Married women usually made great seatmates.

While she was getting settled, one of the flight attendants began to offer orange juice and champagne.

"This is why I like first class," my seatmate announced. "Mimosas are the best way to start the day, don't you think?"

I smiled and nodded my head. I'm much better at writing dialogue than making impromptu conversation with strangers.

"Do you live in Nashville?"

So much for my theory about married women making great seatmates. "No. I'm speaking at a convention."

"In Nashville?"

I bit my tongue since I wanted to reply with something clever, like "No, on Mars." Instead I just nodded my head.

"Will you be staying downtown or at Opryland?"

"Opryland."

"What a coincidence. That's where I'm staying."

"Oh," I managed to say. The flight attendant was taking forever with the champagne.

"I'm going to a wedding."

Nodding my head, I wished I had been seated next to a deaf mute. I contemplated asking her if it was her wedding since she was oozing with the enthusiasm of a bride-to-be.

"What are you speaking about?"

This is why I like what I do for a living. I create characters. And when one of them becomes intolerable, I change them, which is a luxury I don't have with my seatmate.

"Orange juice, champagne or both?" the flight attendant asked the passengers across the aisle.

"I'm speaking about my new book."

"Oh," she replied. "How fabulous. Are you a writer?"

I couldn't believe how I had misjudged her character from my first glance. I was losing my touch. I wanted to admit I was really the Boston strangler. "Yes," I replied, regrettably.

The flight attendant smiled. "Orange juice or champagne?"

"Champagne," my seatmate and I said enthusiastically in unison.

The flight attendant handed us each a plastic glass half filled with champagne.

"I'm Karen," she said, holding her glass in the air.

Nodding my head, I raised my glass. "Cheers." I swallowed a shot of champagne and closed my eyes, hoping the alcohol will quickly put Karen to sleep.

"Have you written anything I might have read?"

It amazed me that Karen could possibly read. Incessant talkers seldom read, or at least that is what I had heard recently on Oprah. I glanced at her and smiled. "What sort of books do you read?"

"Oh, you name it, I've read it. Nicholas Sparks is my favorite."

I cringed. Nicolas Sparks is my biggest competition. "Really?"

"Oh, he's the best. He always writes about places he has lived, and I believe home is where the heart is. He has a way of bringing the reader into his heart, so that you sense the emotion his characters are feeling. Such a passionate writer. I met him once at a book signing in Beverly Hills. Oh, I'm so thrilled you're going to Nashville. You will absolutely love Opryland. Is this your first visit?"

That's when I realized I hadn't been to Nashville in almost thirty years. "No. The last time I was there was back in the seventies. In fact, I went to Opryland then, when it was a theme park." As Karen sipped the rest of her champagne, I hoped she would look out the window, count the bags waiting to be loaded and then fall asleep.

"I remember Opryland back in the seventies. Boy it was something, wasn't it? Then Dolly Parton built Dollywood and before you knew it, everyone was doing a theme park."

Nodding my head, I reached in my pocket for my cell phone. Glancing at it to make sure it was turned on, I never wished more for a phone call to interrupt me than right now. Normally, Jennifer, my publicist, would have called by now to make sure I had made it to the airport, but having missed flights in the past when I was attending speaking engagements or book signing events, she got wise and hired a car to pick me up and get me to the airport on time. That left no excuse for me to miss a flight.

"Sir, we've just closed the entry door," the flight attendant announced as she removed our champagne glasses. "You'll need to turn your phone off and stow it until after we land in Nashville."

I nodded my head, and complied with her request. My last hope for an interruption had vanished.

"Have you been to Monell's?" asked Karen. "It's in Germantown."

"No, I haven't—"

"—Oh, you must go. It's a bit of a drive from Opryland, but well worth the ride. You will think you've died and gone to heaven. I tried to get Carol—the bride's mother—to have them cater the wedding, but she had already selected someone. You have not experienced southern cooking unless you go to Monell's. Shall I write it down for you?"

"Sure." I realize acquiescence is how I am going to survive the next four hours.

Thank goodness American Airlines had the foresight to schedule a movie during the flight. Shortly after take off, while I listened to Karen tell me about her family, the wedding she was attending, every detail of the bridal party and more information than I needed to know about the bride's dress, a flight attendant announced they were about to screen an animated film I had no interest in watching. Even though my head was pounding from consuming two more glasses of champagne, I wanted to drift off to sleep and not wake up until after we had landed in Nashville.

My wish nearly came true. While fast asleep and dreaming of being on a deserted beach in Fiji, Karen needed to use the restroom. Not wanting to awaken me, she carefully maneuvered her way around my seat. Had it not been for a brief bit of rough air that buffeted the jet, she might have succeeded. However, as she was climbing over me, the turbulence caused Karen to lose her balance. As she fell onto me, she grabbed the seat in front of us, plucking the hair extensions right off of the woman's head. Startled by her scalp being yanked, the woman in front of me knocked her coffee mug over, spilling the warm liquid all over her tray table and onto the armrest of the man seated next to her.

Awakened by the simultaneous scream of both women and having the wind knocked out of me as one hundred and twenty pounds of unexpected weight fell on my body, my first thought as I opened my eyes was that our plane had crashed. But when I saw the look of confusion on the face of the flight attendant, I realized the only accident was Karen's attempt to navigate out of her seat.

"What's going on?" asked the flight attendant, authoritatively.

"I was trying to get out so that I could use the restroom," explained Karen, "and I didn't want to waken Will. The plane hit an air pocket and I lost my balance."

The woman in front of me felt the top of her head and turned to discover Karen maintaining a firm grip on her hair extensions.

Realizing the extent of her misfortune, Karen handed the strips of hair to the woman. "I'm very sorry. I didn't mean to—"

"—Is everyone alright?" asked the flight attendant.

I was catatonic. Out of breath and unable to move, I said nothing as Karen straddled my right leg and moved into the aisle. The flight attendant seemed more concerned about the woman in front of me, who needed a hairdresser and paper towels. Instinctively, the flight attendant returned to the galley while the woman found a scarf in her handbag and secured it over her disheveled hair. The man seated next to her, with his arm bathed in warm coffee, was sound asleep, oblivious to what had just happened.

Karen followed the flight attendant and requested another glass of champagne.

After her visit to the restroom, before returning to her seat, Karen explained to the flight crew that had assembled in the forward galley that I was a published author on my way to a huge promotional event and encouraged each of them to get a copy of my new book, even though she had yet to read it. My agent would be happy to know promotion of my novel was alive and well at thirty thousand feet.

❦   ❦   ❦

"I'm curious about how you first discovered Nashville," Karen asked, "and how you managed to stay away for so long?"

By now I realized the only thing subtle about my seatmate was her soft fragrance. Reflecting upon my first visit to Nashville took me back to nineteen seventy-six, when I was approaching the quarter century mark of my life. The closest I had come to visiting the South was a family reunion in St. Louis, Missouri, about two hundred miles north of Nashville. "That was such a long time ago," I said. "A friend of mine was about to begin his last year of medical school in Memphis. I had spent a week with him and he wanted me to visit Nashville before I returned to California. We left Memphis early on a Saturday morning and spent the afternoon at Opryland. I remember how magical it was, between the rides, the animals at the petting zoo, and the food—"

"—Yes, I can imagine how the food must have been a new experience for you."

"Karen, I was in awe. And the people … everyone was so friendly, so unhurried. I remember my first thought was how simple life was there. The rest of the nation seemed somewhat out of control, with protests about equal rights for women, and we were still recovering from the Watergate scandal. Visiting Nashville provided me with a nice respite, and it was a complete departure from the chaos of southern California."

"I can't imagine what you must have thought when you returned to California."

My mind reflected upon that special place in time when life was unhurried … before telephone answering machines, voicemail, the Internet and cell phones forever changed the complexion of the communications industry. "If we could only go back in time," I said.

Karen nodded her head in agreement. "I know."

"There are a few things I would have done differently."

CHAPTER 2

A light snow was falling as the town car headed towards Opryland. I glanced out of the window as the driver negotiated his way towards the expressway. "This is awesome. I feel like I'm on a movie set. The snow is so beautiful."

"The forecast has everyone somewhat concerned," the driver explained. "Hopefully you aren't planning to play golf tomorrow."

I shake my head. "I'm here for a convention. No worries, golf is not on my agenda, although a long nap would be nice."

"Where did you fly in from?"

"California, where people have no clue how to drive in the snow."

The song on the car radio concluded as the announcer mentioned a disco reunion party scheduled at a club in downtown Nashville before he segued to a play list of older disco tunes, beginning with "The Hustle."

"Wow. I haven't heard this in a while. I think it's been about thirty years since 'The Hustle' was born.

"Are you going to be around next weekend?" asked the driver.

"No. I'm heading to Chicago on Sunday."

"Too bad. There's a big disco party downtown. It should be 'Saturday Night Fever' all over again."

I nodded my head as I glanced at the driver in the rear view mirror. "Sorry I'm going to miss it."

"I hear John Travolta is flying in for the event."

I took comfort knowing I wasn't the only person having to sell myself in Nashville. As the beat of the song reverberated from the speakers, I was temporarily transported to a time when I was heavily influenced by music ... when I felt like a dove in a field of hawks. During the nineteen seventies, I found refuge in the world these songs portrayed, which forgave indifference and pro-moted peace and diversity … not bigotry, discrimination or war. While many of my friends formulated their sense of perception with the help of recreational drugs, my stream of consciousness followed the lyric of many songs that were popular at the time.

As the song ended, my driver approached the entrance to Opryland. I observed a tall structure off in the distance. The hotel had the appearance of a large corporate office building with a massive glass-domed ceiling. It was not the look I expected for the largest hotel-convention complex in Tennessee. Minutes later, as the town car pulled up to the hotel's main entrance, the loom-ing structure became larger than life.

Passing through the revolving glass doors, I was thrust into a massive lobby surrounded by a summer-like theme park. While it was snowing outside, the inside temperature at Opryland was set at sixty-eight degrees year-round. A multi-story waterfall across from the entryway cascaded tons of recycled water that filled lagoons and a river walk surrounding the interior of the multi-story three-thousand-room hotel. A riverboat filled with guests slowly passed by. From the helm of the boat, the captain waved at the throng of people in the lobby.

The tranquility of the moment suspended my consciousness. As I inhaled the aroma of the faux river water, surrounded by the sound of Nashville's "Nia-gara Falls," a dozen people passed by me to join the registration line, which snaked through the lobby. Resembling an airline ticket counter on the day before Thanksgiving, I glanced at my watch. I had one hour before I needed to be at the cocktail reception hosted by my publisher.

"Good evening, Mr. Taylor." said the Concierge as the doorman led me to the corner of the registration desk. "We have pre-registered you in a lovely suite in the Magnolia Court. I'll have your bags sent up to your suite. Here is your entry card and a map detailing how to find your way through the hotel. It's really very simple. Just follow the signs leading you to the Magnolia Court beyond the escalator," said the Concierge, pointing towards a rain forest.

"Thank you." I noticed the Concierge's nametag, which read *Bob, Dickson, Tennessee.* "You're from Dickson?"

"Yes," replied the Concierge.

"I have an old friend from there. Actually, I *had* a friend from there."

"It's only about forty-five minutes from here. When I first came to work at Opryland, I heard it took longer for some guests to find their rooms than it took me to get home to Dickson."

I nodded my head as the Concierge handed me the map. "Just follow the signs?"

"Yes, Mr. Taylor. I've highlighted in green the path you should follow. It's not that hard, really.

"Thanks Bob." Every corner of the hotel had a themed name, which reminded me of Disneyland.

"I hope you enjoy your stay with us."

Walking along the river walk towards the escalator, I glanced up at the atrium ceiling and noticed the snow falling far above me. Opryland had created the illusion of being surrounded by summer when, in fact, it was the middle of winter.

Twenty minutes later I arrived at the Magnolia Court. My journey from the registration area near "Niagara Nashville" took me up two flights of moving stairs to the Cascades, a cross between Austin, Texas and New Orleans. From there I walked past the Old Hickory Steakhouse to the entrance of the convention center. The Magnolia Court was just beyond the entrance to Delta Island, featuring an assortment of shops and a food court.

Finally I reached my suite. My luggage had already arrived. I glanced at the bedside alarm clock which illuminated the time: Five twenty. I had forty minutes before the cocktail reception was scheduled to begin. I kicked off my shoes and stretched across the bed, closing my eyes for a quick power nap.

❦   ❦   ❦

At seven o'clock, my publicist telephoned my suite. The ringing of the telephone awakened me.

"Hello?"

"Will, please tell me you're not asleep."

"How could I be asleep when I'm talking to you?"

"Do not make me go up there and drag you down here."

"Give me ten minutes."

"You promise?"

"I promise."

"I'm counting," Jennifer said, impatiently.

Writers on deadline can usually perform a written miracle in a matter of minutes. But the same time constraints don't work so well when we are forced to make personal appearances. I got up and reached for my suitcase, opening it slowly. Jennifer would probably compare my slow movements to those from

"Gone With The Wind" when Scarlett O'Hara's maid, Prissy, went searching for a doctor after Melanie went into labor.

Since the clock was ticking, I decided against taking a quick shower. I washed my face, brushed my teeth, and slicked back my hair to give it the appearance that I had just showered. Changing into a new button down dress shirt, I grabbed a jacket from my garment bag and headed to the cocktail reception.

The Old Hickory Steakhouse is housed in what is described in the hotel brochure as an old plantation mansion located along the river walk. I quickly realized the plantation house was merely a façade. As I approached the foyer, the laughter and loud conversation emanating from the reception made me nervous. I felt like I was arriving at a party where everyone was several drinks ahead of me.

A very attractive woman at the entryway smiled and I instantly felt better. "Are you here for the reception?"

"Yes."

She glanced down at the guest list. "May I have your last name?"

"Taylor."

Looking up, she beamed. "Will?"

I nodded my head and flashed a smile.

"Oh. *You're* Will Taylor," she said with a welcoming southern accent. "You look much better than your publicity photo."

"Thanks." I glanced around the crowded room. "I'm looking for my publicist."

"She's over there," said the woman, pointing towards the bar. "By the way, I'm Brenda."

"It's nice to meet a friendly face."

"I hope you all have a wonderful time in Nashville."

I nodded my head as I glanced towards the bar, where Jennifer was surrounded by a group of people. As our eyes connected, I saw the look of relief on her face. I slowly made my way to the group surrounding her as she began to introduce everyone to me. I smiled, nodding my head as I was introduced to each person, shaking their hand and telling them how happy I was to meet them.

This continued for nearly two hours. I had no idea so many people liked my work. It felt good to be acknowledged, but as good as that feeling was, I was pining for a good night's sleep in my suite.

As I attempted to make my way towards the entrance, three women in their sixties surrounded Jennifer, each holding a copy of my new book. The look of desperation on Jenn's face begged me to help rescue her. I walked towards them and reached for the pen from my jacket pocket. "Hello ladies. How are all of you doing on this magnificent night?"

"Oh my God, it's really him," said one of the women.

"It's a magnificent night because you arrived," said another one of the women.

"I told you he would make it," said Jennifer. "Will, I would like to introduce you to three of your biggest fans."

As Jenn introduced me to the women, I glanced across the river walk to a beautiful rotunda situated alongside a waterfall. Lilies draped the area that was being set up for a wedding. For a brief second my mind flashed to a wedding I had attended years earlier in the lush gardens of Hawaii. Ben Stiller had invited me to attend his wedding to actress Christine Taylor along "Secret Beach" on the island of Kauai. It was magical, not only because of being surrounded by the lush, tropical paradise of the Hawaiian Islands, but because love was very much in the air. Glancing at the rotunda, where cloth-covered chairs were being arranged near the cascading waterfall, I felt momentarily transported back to the Taylor-Stiller wedding.

"Will?" said Jennifer, interrupting my gaze.

"Yes?"

"These ladies would like you to sign their books."

"Of course. Who would like to be first?"

All three women raised their hands as they handed me their newly purchased copies of my novel.

❧   ❧   ❧

After wishing everyone a good night, Jennifer and I walked along the river walk towards the Magnolia Court.

"Is there anything you need for tomorrow?" Jenn asked.

"No … thanks. I'm all set."

"The tourism convention is hosting an event at the Grand Ole Opry tomorrow night. They extended an invitation for you to attend."

I gave Jenn a look that said 'Thanks, but no thanks.'

"Will, for as much grief as I give you, you really are a pleasure to work with."

"And all this time I thought I was high maintenance."

"Trust me. You're so *not* that. Habitually late, maybe, but not high maintenance. I remember our first meeting.

"That was several novels ago."

"Yes. San Francisco. We were doing a mock interview at the new Barnes and Noble in Union Square."

"I wasn't late for that, was I?"

"No. You were on time. But you were so shy. I thought we were going to lose you when that crusty old man stood up and asked you how much money writers made."

"I forgot what my answer was."

"You told him you didn't have a clue. But whatever it was, it wasn't enough."

"That sounds like what I would have said."

"You were so accommodating. The store manager couldn't believe you had never done a book signing before."

"I hate to make you earn your salary, Jenn, but was tonight a success?"

"Will, are you kidding me? Each of the people that came paid one hundred dollars for the chance to meet you."

"That's ridiculous. No one should have to pay. They should just come to my book signing tomorrow … for free."

"It's not like that for these people. They want some private one-on-one time. Haven't you ever wanted to meet a singer and not have to share that moment with a bunch of groupies?"

I thought for a moment. "No."

"Will, you've led a very sheltered life. It's perfectly normal for people who enjoy someone's passion, whether it's art, music, or writing … to spend a few minutes with that artist to better understand what they're about."

"Do you think everyone who came tonight better understands who Will Taylor is?"

Jenn was reflective. "Yes, I do. You were present. You spoke with everyone. You signed books. You made conversation. That's all that people want … a little interaction. Unfortunately, this is all part of being a successful writer."

We reached the lobby of the Magnolia Court. "Well, right now it's all about a date with me and my bed."

"Sleep well, Will. I'll call you in the morning."

As I began to remind her, Jenn put her hand on my shoulder.

"Not to worry. I won't call before ten."

"Thanks," I said as I hugged her.

"Night, Will."

Walking towards my suite, I reflected back to the first time I visited Nashville. Dolly Parton headlined at the Grand Ole Opry. Minnie Pearl was still
alive. Music Row was a sight to behold. I smiled as I reminisced. Although I am
not a fan of country music, Nashville is a most welcoming city.

Once in my suite, I hung my jacket in the bedroom closet and took off my
clothes. Lacking the energy to unpack, I climbed into bed and savored the
crisp, freshly laundered sheets under the down comforter. My head and the pil-
low united like long lost friends, and as I drifted off to sleep, my mind flashed
back to something that was missing in my life.

CHAPTER 3

During the summer of nineteen seventy-five, I was hired as a reservations agent for Continental Airlines. It was a great job for a twenty-three-year-old. One that paid very well, with travel benefits that allowed me to go places during my time off that I would not have been able to afford to visit without the perks of my job. Many of my college friends had not yet been to Europe, but I had already traveled to Amsterdam, Copenhagen, London, Paris and Tokyo. Because of my airline pass benefits, I could fly for free and get discounts at hotels all over the world. The only thing missing in my life was someone to explore the world with.

The airline industry was about to begin a tumultuous period signified by the end of many years of tradition regulated by the highly controversial Civil Aeronautics Board ("the CAB"). Under pressure from new entrants who wanted to share in the wealth, Congress debated proposed legislation that eventually led to the deregulation of the airline industry. In nineteen seventy-five, before the CAB was abolished, a passenger knew which airline to contact when booking a reservation based on their point of origination and destination. The airlines controlled their markets based on the approval of the CAB, and Continental was an airline that flourished under the CAB's regulation.

Profitability was determined by the routes an airline was awarded, and fare structures became complicated when competing carriers served the same market. Many of Continental's markets were unmatched by other carriers, which made those routes an untapped gold mine. Providing a unique passenger experience in the competitive markets they served required Continental to be innovative in marketing their product and providing customer service that was better than American, TWA or United. Armed with a unique corporate identity—a golden sunburst on the tail of every aircraft—Continental developed a slick advertising campaign that promised their employees would "really move our tail for you." With frequent billboard, magazine, radio and television advertising, Continental had become known as "the proud bird with the golden tail." It was also the only airline that had a Polynesian pub on every wide-bodied aircraft. Passengers preferred flying Continental over the competition because the in-flight service was an exceptional experience provided by no other airline.

During the mid-nineteen seventies, the air traveler was also more sophisticated and well mannered. Travel by air was an experience that one enjoyed rather than endured. Regrettably, deregulation of the airline industry eventually changed all of that. In between providing schedule and fare information and booking reservations for passengers, I spent considerable time day-dreaming about becoming a part of the elite corps of men and women who wore designer uniforms and traveled all over the world.

The seventies also produced the beginning of another controversial change in America: the sexual revolution. Women fought for equal rights in the work place, and within the airline industry—especially the in-flight arena—the work place became a battleground for equality. Previously, flight attendants were referred to as stewardesses. Even the call button above passenger seats had the outline of a woman. It was not considered a career for men. Many airlines were forced to eliminate weight restrictions for this group of employees, which had always been discriminately implemented, along with age limits and the requirement that a stewardess resign if she were to get married. Because of a variety of changes to the work rules that were implemented through the collective bargaining process, Continental began to hire male flight attendants to help balance their workforce. As a result of a mass recruitment effort that began in the mid-seventies, many of my male co-workers in the reservations department applied to transfer to in-flight service. While the base pay was much less than working in reservations, the time off was incredible (ranging from eleven to fourteen days each month), and the potential of additional flight time pay meant one could earn more by flying all over the country serving drinks and meals than sitting in an office booking reservations for strangers that would become passengers in the sky. And they could fly with all of these good-looking women.

After hearing about the grueling group interview process from several of my co-workers, I was dared by these guys to send my application to the recruitment office. "They'll never hire you," said Marc, a very tall yet slightly built guy with a dark complexion who lived in Long Beach. "They want jocks, not swimmers." At least that was what he believed after not getting invited back for a second interview. Marc and I had talked about how cool it would be to fly all over the country, and I figured I had nothing to lose. "Go ahead, Will," he said one afternoon. "Send in your application and when they see you live at the beach, you won't get invited for an interview. You're not what they're looking for," he said, rather matter-of-factly.

Reluctantly, I sent in my application. A week later, I received a letter inviting me to attend a group interview at Continental's general office, a couple of miles from the reservations complex. Excited about the potential of flying all over the country, my enthusiasm was diminished when a few more of my co-workers who had previously been invited to participate in flight attendant group interviews received letters of rejection from the recruiter. Apparently getting hired as a flight attendant was not as easy as it sounded.

I was nervous when I entered the lobby of the general office, where over two dozen guys around my age were assembled. All dressed in business attire, some of the applicants had flown in from other parts of the country, courtesy of Continental. Most of them looked like they had played football in high school, something foreign to me as I spent my afternoons in high school running cross country and surfing. Feeling slightly vulnerable, I quickly realized how keen the competition was. I nervously glanced at my watch. It was a few minutes before two o'clock. I contemplated making a run for it when a side door opened and a woman with short dark blonde hair wearing a suit with a very short skirt and platform pumps appeared. "Hello, gentlemen," she said authoritatively. "Welcome to Continental. We're going to be conducting our group interview in the flight training center just across the parking lot. Please follow me."

The conference room had been configured with a circle of folding chairs. Anita Elliott, the in-flight service recruiter, stood to the side accompanied by an assistant with a steno pad, recording everything that happened. They were both polished and professional. After a short introduction about the rigors of becoming a flight attendant, Ms. Elliott painted a rather less than attractive picture of the training process, which consisted of six weeks of unpaid classroom instruction in Los Angeles that required a ninety percent pass rate for every examination. Each Friday, flight attendant candidates would take a written exam that would determine whether or not the candidate continued their training. At the end of the five weeks, an over-water ditching exercise observed by representatives of the FAA served as the final exam. At any point of the training process, if a flight attendant candidate was late for class or failed to score at least ninety percent, they would be sent home. Provided a flight attendant candidate passed the vigorous training and successfully completed a thorough background check conducted by the FBI, the assignment to a home base would occur at the graduation ceremony. This assignment would be based on seniority and the company's crew requirements. The flight attendant bases included Chicago, Denver, El Paso, Houston and Los Angeles; however, the Chicago flight attendant base was being closed, and most of the flight attendants based there were transferring to either Denver or Los Angeles, which meant my chances of remaining in Los Angeles were very much up in the air.

With that, Ms. Elliott invited everyone to share something about themselves with the group, suggesting they talk about why they wanted to become a flight attendant, and what working for Continental meant to them. My co-workers had given me pointers about the group interview process. "Don't wait until the end to speak. They like assertive people. Don't mention your airline experience. They want guys who have no experience. Don't look at the interviewers. Eye contact with the group is important." I was overwhelmed with all of the advice. Then I heard Marc's voice, telling me I'd never get invited for an interview since I wasn't what they were looking for. And here I was, looking at the face of my future.

"Who wants to be first?" asked Ms. Elliott, glancing in my direction. I smiled but didn't move. I was thinking about the selection of flight attendant bases and the possibility I might have to move to Texas when the first candidate stood up and introduced himself. This process continued for about forty-five minutes. Each time I developed the courage to stand, someone else beat me to it. Halfway through the group, a nice looking guy with dark curly hair from San Diego stood up and talked about how he wanted to be hired because he could really move his tail for Continental. Everyone laughed. I thought he was pretty clever.

Finally, everyone but me had spoken. "Anyone else?" asked Ms. Elliott, again glancing at me. Reluctantly, I stood up. "Hi. My name is Will. I live in Newport Beach and I currently work for Continental. It's such a great company, and I'm proud to be a part of this team. I want to be a flight attendant because our passengers deserve an experience they will remember, and hopefully share with others. It's about making their flight something special. Thank you." I looked at a few of the guys while I spoke, but I remember smiling at Anita Elliott when I talked about working for Continental.

After I sat down, I was horrified because I did everything wrong. I mentioned Newport Beach, which was in Orange County. Having resigned two years earlier, our country's former president, Richard Nixon, was living in exile a few miles from my apartment. Southern California—especially Orange County—resided in a state of shame. And here I was touting where I lived as confidently as the fact that I worked for the proud bird with the golden tail. My chances of being invited back for a second interview were slim to none.

When I returned to work, everyone wanted to know how the interview went. As I relayed all of the things I did wrong, no one gave me any hope. "You went last?" asked Peter, a guy who worked on the rate desk. "You're doomed, buddy."

The following week, I received a letter inviting me back for a second interview. During this meeting, which lasted about twenty minutes, Ms. Elliot asked me how I liked the group interview. I told her it was somewhat of a challenge.

"Whom do you remember from that day?" she asked.

I reflected back to the others there that afternoon and envisioned the guy with dark curly hair from San Diego. "I remember the applicant who said he would really move his tail for Continental if he got hired," I said, enthusiastically.

"Oh, dear God," said Anita. "I thought he was so full of himself."

My face went blank. "Well, he had charisma," I said, somewhat chagrined.

Anita nodded her head as she looked over my employment application. "Yes, he did have that."

Following a series of questions about hypothetical situations that required me to evaluate how I might react while flying thousands of miles above ground, Anita asked me when I might be available to return and meet with the senior vice president of in-flight service. Following that meeting I would need to visit the company's medical department for a physical examination.

I left Continental's general office feeling as if I was soaring at thirty-two thousand feet. A week later, following my subsequent interview and medical exam, I reported for work in the reservations office. "Hey Will," said Marc as I clocked in. "You seem like you're in a good mood. You must have gone surfing this morning."

I was beaming when I announced I was accepted as a candidate for Continental's third in-flight service class of the year, scheduled to commence a few weeks later.

Becoming a flight attendant was the most exciting thing in my life, and I was not the least bit concerned about the training, since becoming a reservations agent required learning a lot of abbreviations and codes, all of which were transferable skills. The most important aspect of becoming a flight attendant was mastering the emergency and safety procedures, which were largely based on common sense and reacting in a timely fashion. So my six weeks of training flew by, and I graduated in late April to be awarded my first choice of home base assignment: Los Angeles.

For the next two months, I was assigned to reserve status, which meant I was on stand by to cover flights when other flight attendants called in sick or were unavailable because of vacation or operational need. Most of the flights I was assigned to cover were to and from Chicago on wide-body aircraft. By the end of June, I was able to hold a regular schedule, knowing when and where I would be traveling. And for the month of July, I managed to have the first three days of the month off, although I had to check-in at eleven o'clock on the eve of July Fourth.

The Bicentennial Fourth of July had become a monumental celebration for the entire nation. For several weeks, Jane Pauley and Bryant Gumbel—hosts of the *Today Show*—had been promoting the myriad of events scheduled throughout the country. Since the holiday landed on a Monday, most everyone was planning a long weekend celebration. Many of my friends had scheduled trips to Boston, New York and San Francisco, where major historic events were scheduled.

I called my friend Marc to see if he wanted to do something. As always, his phone rang without an answer. Marc was never home. Since transferring to in-flight service, Marc and I saw much less of one another. The only thing we shared in common while working in reservations was our love of surfing and an intrigue of one another. Now that I was a flight attendant with a different schedule than his, the only thing we had in common was living at the beach.

On Friday evening I decided to drive up to West Hollywood. The assortment of people my own age at Studio One, the west coast's premiere disco, was abundant, and the music and sound system was just what I needed, because entering the club as the music blared helped diffuse my discomfort of being in a predominantly gay club. Walking into Studio One was only palatable because no one could hear my heart pounding in fear that someone might look at me and surmise I was gay.

Entering the club, I instantly got lost in the moment. I didn't feel self-conscious because the lights were so dim and the dominant music captured my attention. In my mind, the focus was never about the person entering the club. But with my diminished vision and thumping heart, I was unaware that all eyes were focused on me.

Studio One was housed in a cavernous barn-like building. I had previously visited less than half a dozen times—the last time a few weeks earlier when my friend Timmy introduced me to "The Back Lot" (a cabaret located on the second floor with an entrance at the rear of the club where a chanteuse was performing). The singer captured my breath as well as the attention of the audience with her deeply passionate interpretation of a variety of torch songs that I had never heard before. Her name was Jane Olivor, and she ended her set with an arrangement of "Some Enchanted Evening," which moved me to tears. The thought of discovering someone who might find me attractive and worthy was simply beyond my wildest imagination. After all, I was gay ... yet the lyric gave me some semblance of hope for the future. And the singer's interpretation molded my hope into a perception of reality that promised it might be possible to find a long and lasting love.

The cover to get into Studio One had just gone up to two bucks. To help defray the expense of the entrance fee, I parked on a side street a couple of blocks away. The alternative was to spend three dollars to park in the public lot. Not having to shell out three bucks to park meant I could have a second beer.

My long sun-bleached hair bobbed from side to side as I sprinted up the steps. Entering the club, my sparkling white teeth shined against my dark tan. A few weeks earlier when I visited Studio One, Timmy told me I was a head turner. While I disagreed, he put things in perspective. "Will, at five feet ten, your slender frame and natural good looks causes people to notice you." However, I didn't even notice anyone looking at me as I walked into the club, since I came from a world where being gay was non-existent.

Walking past the front bar, I entered the main floor where the gigantic sound system pounded hard against my body. A couple of guys glanced towards me, but I sensed they could tell I was from Orange County and really didn't belong there. I guess I had what some psychologists would diagnose as low self-esteem. It was not easy being me.

As I made my way onto the main floor, I observed guys lined up against the wall which reminded me of a school dance—without the girls. I knew I was not going to get picked because I didn't dance, so I walked hurriedly through the disco and headed towards the bar located at the rear of the main floor.

I reached the bar and noticed a handsome Mediterranean-looking guy with dark hair leaning against the bar. Our eyes met as he flashed a huge smile. Although he was totally my type, I looked away. A moment later, I glanced back towards him and smiled, then looked away, again. "Boy is he cute," I thought to myself.

Trying to get the bartender's attention, I felt someone approaching me. I glanced over my shoulder to find the cute guy with dark hair standing next to me.

"Want to dance?" he asked.

"I don't dance," I replied with an embarrassed look.

As he reached for my hand, Adam flashed a smile that melted my heart. "It's no big deal."

CHAPTER 4

As we reached the edge of the dance floor, "The Hustle" began to play.

"Oh, no … please not this," I said, shaking my head. "I can't do 'The Hustle.'"

"Come on," said Adam, reaching for my hand. "We'll do this together."

I followed his lead as couples brushed past us, descending on to the dance floor. Surrounded by people with coordinated choreography, Adam and I found ourselves in a world of our own. It didn't matter that the cadence of the song required each step to be impeccably orchestrated in perfect rhythm. We moved at our own pace and marched to the beat of an absent drummer. Adam's smile reassured me that everything was alright. Even though right off the bat I bumped into the couple near us on the edge of the dance floor, the twinkle in Adam's eyes comforted me. He made our attempt to do "The Hustle" seem effortless. While I tried to emulate his movements, I failed miserably; however, Adam made me feel as if I had been transported to another planet. Had it not been for him, I would never have gained the confidence to make an appearance on the huge dance floor. Each time that I began to feel self conscious, I would look at Adam. The nod of his head coupled with his smile reassured me and gave me a sense of security that everything was okay. As I glanced into his eyes, I could see forever. It felt like I was flying above the clouds where everything was so beautiful and clear … and I could see such happiness in Adam's beautiful eyes. For the first time in my life, I wasn't uncomfortable dancing with a man. In fact, it felt rather nice … almost natural.

It was ironic that this stranger had come into my life, providing me with a safety net to try "The Hustle" when none of my friends were willing to teach me the steps. "How did you manage to learn this?" I asked him.

"I was a cheerleader in college," Adam explained. "Dance moves are easy to learn," he said, confidently.

Maybe dance moves were easy for him, but they were anything but easy for me. I was in awe of this guy and wondered why I was the fortunate one he tapped on the shoulder and asked to dance. We remained inseparable for two more songs, checking each other out, before the Three Degrees song "When Will I See You Again?" pounded through the sound system.

"Where do you live?" asked Adam as the song ended.

"Newport Beach," I replied flashing a huge smile.

"Is that close by?" he asked with a slight southern accent.

"You're not from here, are you?"

Adam shook his head in embarrassment.

"It's about an hour away," I explained. "Are you visiting family or friends?"

Adam nodded his head. "I'm staying with a friend in Silverlake. "You're welcome to spend the night there if you want."

"Okay," I said without hesitation. "My truck is only a couple of blocks from here."

As we made our way through Studio One, Adam spotted his friend, Neal, and signaled that he was leaving with me. "I don't want Neal to think I've been kidnapped."

"Does that happen to you often?" I asked.

Adam gave me a reassuring look. "This is my first trip to California," he explained. "I didn't know what to expect. Neal told me Studio One was the place anyone who visits must experience, but I didn't anticipate meeting someone as cute as you."

I recoiled. The word cute was how most people described me. I hated it. Cute was what girls were supposed to be. I was a guy. Handsome, virile, strong, good-looking … those were adjectives I yearned would be used to describe me. Adam was all of the above. But apparently, I was … cute.

❋   ❋   ❋

Having spent my entire life in southern California, it was somewhat ironic there were parts of Los Angeles that I did not know even existed. The Silverlake district, located east of Los Angeles and south of the San Gabriel Valley, was one of those places. Adam, on the other hand, had such a keen sense of direction and knew exactly how to get to his friend's apartment from West Hollywood. Providing copious directions, I was thrilled to have Adam sitting next to me. It was a refreshing departure from the other times I had met someone at Studio One and followed their car through the dark neighborhoods of West Hollywood for what amounted to be a single night rendezvous. Glancing at him, I was drawn to Adam's defined body and I found his southern drawl intriguing.

While driving to Silverlake, Adam explained that he lived in Memphis and was visiting his friend, Neal, who had just graduated from the same medical school where Adam would begin his final year next month.

"I'm a medical student," Adam explained when I asked what he was studying.

"Wow. That is so wild. Are you going to become a doctor?"

"That's the plan," said Adam, nonchalantly.

He was not very enthusiastic as he explained that he had enrolled in the ROTC program that paved the way for his future career in the medical profession. Through the ROTC, Adam was provided a scholarship to attend both undergraduate and medical school. While both of us had avoided serving in the Vietnam War because we attended accredited universities, the difference between us was Adam had a full scholarship because of his high grade point average. Little did I know I was going home with a bon vivant genius.

Once we arrived at Neal's small apartment, I was relieved to discover their relationship was platonic as Adam's sleeping bag dominated most of the living room. He motioned for me to join him on the fleece lining and soon after I did, our lips met. Kissing him was the most magical moment of the night, something we did until we both fell asleep, wrapped around one another.

I awakened in Adam's arms and was surprised to find myself not wanting to leave. Usually spending the night with a guy meant I would awaken the next morning regretting my decision and wishing I could magically disappear. I never felt a sense of belonging the morning after; instead, the desire to leave as quickly as possible overcame me. I seldom stayed for coffee and always declined going out for breakfast the next morning. My friend Timmy, on the other hand, was an expert on one-night stands. He even kept a toothbrush and comb in the glove compartment of his car. Unlike Timmy, I always found myself wanting to erase the fact that I had spent the night in the first place and pretend nothing had happened. The morning after was usually met with a sense of regret for me. Glancing over at the guy who looked pretty good after a couple of beers the night before became the least ugly person the next morning. However, this particular Saturday morning I awoke with a much different feeling. Watching Adam as he slept, I wanted very much to stay and learn more about this dark-haired wonder. His breathing was rhythmic, and as I watched him I became aroused.

Adam opened his eyes to find me staring at him. "Hey," he said, flashing his handsome smile.

"Good morning."

He raised his hand and brushed it through my hair. "How is it you're so good-looking in the morning, too?"

I shrugged my shoulders as he kissed me.

"Can we spend the day together?" he asked.

Normally I would have invented an excuse to leave. But being with Adam sparked a much different feeling, and even though he was visiting from Memphis, I didn't want to miss the chance of getting to know him better. He was so full of life that I took a leap of faith and agreed to spend the day with him. I asked him what he wanted to do. He talked about his excursions during the past few days, which included a full day at Disneyland, panning for gold and a visit to Universal Studios. Adam wanted to explore the beaches of southern California, something missing in Memphis. Explaining the geographic layout of Los Angeles, I suggested we drive along the southern California coastline, from Malibu to Laguna Beach (the "gay Mecca" of southern California) and spend the night at my apartment in Newport Beach. Adam quickly packed his things in his duffel bag and wrote a note for Neal, thanking him for letting him stay at his place.

I had never met anyone who had a duffel bag. "What does 'ROTC' stand for?"

"Reserve Officer Training Corps," replied Adam.

"Does that mean you're in the Army?"

Adam nodded his head. "After I graduate from medical school I'll serve my time at a military hospital."

Luck of the draw had kept me from being drafted. However Adam, despite his incredible intellect and full scholarship that would have spared him from the draft, had voluntarily enlisted. "Why the ROTC?"

"It's a long story." Adam leaned over and kissed me. "We'll talk about it later," he said as he tossed the duffel bag over his shoulder. "Come on, Will. Show me these famous beaches I've heard so much about."

Leaving Neal's apartment, I realized this guy from Memphis was much more than a one-night stand. As we headed towards Malibu Canyon, I asked him what made him decide to visit California. Adam explained he had just finished his third year of medical school and was about to begin another term. His whole life had been planned out for him, and he was feeling slightly overwhelmed by it all. Just before the end of the school year, as many of his friends were planning to leave Memphis for the summer, Adam realized he needed a break. California and Hawaii were two places he had always wanted to visit, and two of his closest friends, Linda and Stephen, managed to get enough of his friends to pitch in and pay for a plane ticket.

I was not surprised that Adam had a great group of friends, and I was impressed by how quickly they rallied to help him get away to enjoy a respite in California. As he talked about his desire to travel and explore places he had dreamt about, I reflected upon an elderly woman who sat behind me when I had flown to Hawaii a few months earlier. She explained to her traveling companion how disappointed she was not to have made the trip with her husband while he was alive because it was a trip they had always talked about. Somehow it just never happened. He had recently died following a massive heart attack, and the woman decided to go to Hawaii with her friend to accomplish what she and her husband never did. Listening to the woman tell the story, I felt a certain sadness for her not to be able to share this experience with her husband, and then I realized how important it was to live in the moment and do something you have always dreamed of doing now … for tomorrow may be too late.

Hearing Adam talk about making his wish to visit California come true, I was struck by my good fortune to have crossed paths with him, because I had met someone who was not afraid of adventure. Driving through Topanga Canyon towards Malibu, Adam told me he was "on the mend" from a breakdown. Too much pressure from his father to excel in medical school coupled with a heavy course load while trying to balance all of his scholastic obligations with wanting to socialize with his friends took its toll on Adam. He seemed totally in control while he shared his dilemma, and I sensed he was a young man in charge of his life. After all, he could do "The Hustle" and was about to become a medical doctor. I was just a flight attendant who had visions of becoming a journalist.

I drove to the top of a bluff and parked across the street from a lot that had been cleared for construction. Stakes with flags marked where the foundation would soon be poured. Together we walked through the lot and imagined where each room of the house would be. We envisioned the kitchen would face east, followed by the dining room. The living room would command the center of the house, with a guest bedroom off to the north. We found the perfect spot for the master bedroom and spread out a couple of beach towels that I kept in my truck. As we sat and looked out at the massive Pacific Ocean below us, the fact that I had discovered a panoramic view had Adam tongue-tied. He couldn't imagine how such a remarkable view could possibly exist. I was thrilled at my good fortune to discover such a great spot and felt honored to borrow the location of what would very soon become a million dollar home. For the next few hours, Adam and I were residents of the bluff and enjoyed the unobstructed view from high atop Malibu Canyon.

We both felt as if we were in heaven. Surrounded by a warm ocean breeze, we basked in the warmth of the late morning sun. I leaned over and kissed Adam, thinking that no one could see us, when, in fact, everyone on the surrounding bluff had a bird's eye view. It really didn't matter to either of us since we felt what we were doing was perfectly right. How could it not be? One kiss led to another, and eventually, both of us began to remove our clothes. As we lay completely naked under the warm mid-day sun, I admitted I was not experienced in having sex outdoors. Adam reassured me that was a good thing, since neither was he.

❦   ❦   ❦

"When I told you I had a breakdown, were you worried?" Adam asked me as I handed him a soda from my backpack.

"Concerned that your head might explode," I said. "I can't imagine what it's like studying to become a doctor."

Adam popped open the soda, took a sip and set the can in the sand beside him. He looked at me with his piercing brown eyes and flashed his trademark smile. "You're the first person to actually get how difficult it is."

I put my arm around his shoulders and kissed him. "I can't even imagine how hard it must be."

Adam looked out at the ocean as a warm breeze buffeted the beach grass which surrounded us. The flags marking the perimeter of the house flapped in the wind. "I wasn't sure I could go through with it."

"Go through with what?" I asked.

"Finishing medical school."

I watched as Adam took another sip of his soda. "After finishing the term exams, I didn't think I was going to pass, so I came home and took a couple of pills. Muscle relaxants they prescribed after I strained my shoulder from playing tennis. Then I took a few more. As I began to feel sleepy, I took the rest of the pills."

I stared at the ocean. "How many pills did you take?"

"Enough to kill me."

I couldn't believe I was listening to a bright, articulate, handsome man, who appeared to have everything going for him, tell me he had attempted to kill himself.

"Fortunately, my brain was still wide awake. And it was screaming at me to call someone. So I called my roommate at work, but he was in a meeting." Adam took another sip of soda. "Then I called my guidance counselor, but she had left early that day. So I called a friend of mine who works at the medical school. She could tell right away something was wrong. First thing she asked me was where I was, and I told her. She told me to go unlock the front door. I said I would when we were finished. Linda was so calm, and she firmly told me to get up and unlock the door. So I did."

"Thank God," I said, leaning my head against his shoulder.

"While I was unlocking the door, Linda was telling her secretary to call the police and request an ambulance be dispatched to my house."

"It sounds like you've got some really great friends."

"I do, Will. Without them, I probably would not be here right now."

I was in a state of disbelief as Adam took the last sip of his soda. He must have sensed my discomfort, as he changed the subject. "What's that amusement park over there?" he asked.

"The Santa Monica Pier. We can stop there next, if you want."

"How far away is Laguna Beach?" he asked.

"It's a little over an hour from here."

He leaned over and kissed me.

"I'm glad you're here," I said.

"Thank God I met you," Adam replied.

CHAPTER 5

In the warmth of the afternoon sun, we descended Malibu Canyon and headed towards Santa Monica.

Adam was in awe of the natural beauty of the vast coastline and displayed the enthusiasm of a kid at Christmas as the panoramic view of the Pacific extended across the horizon for as far as we could see. I enjoyed the way he marveled at the natural beauty of southern California, something I had become nonplussed with having grown up at the beach. What I was taken by was having met such a good-looking guy my own age that was effortless fun to be around.

In the short time since we had first met, I was drawn to Adam in a way that I had never experienced before. Most guys had an agenda. It was always about having sex. For some primitive reason, it seemed important to others to sleep with as many people as possible, almost as if there was a contest to see who achieved the highest score. After I became a flight attendant, it got even worse. The straight guys I flew with were continually trying to get me to score with ladies they had been unable to hook up with, and most of the ones who were gay were all about sleeping with every male flight attendant on the Continental system. I found it easier to just keep to myself on layovers and not hang out with the crew, which only confused many of my colleagues since no one could quite figure me out. "Is Will straight or gay?" was the question many crew-members asked after flying a trip with me. The only self-imposed rule I made when I graduated from flight attendant training was never to sleep with a passenger. I guess you could say Will Taylor considered a career as a flight attendant more than a chance to meet people for sexual liaisons. My best friends would tell you I had good moral character.

Adam was a refreshing change as he didn't appear to have a score card. He impressed me as someone who was more about enjoying life and savoring the moment. He had such a lust for life that it was infectious to be around him, and I yearned to learn more about who he was.

Driving down to Laguna Beach was much easier with someone else in the truck to keep me company. And the long drive afforded me a chance to explore more about my new friend. While driving along Pacific Coast Highway, which intersected the beginning of Interstate Ten, I asked Adam if he was enjoying himself.

"Will, little did I know when I came here to pan for gold that I would find a gold mine," he said, flashing a huge smile. "I knew it was going to be a trip I would never forget. I just wish I had met you when I first arrived."

I nodded my head and flashed him a smile, relieved to hear he felt the same way I did.

"Have you ever panned for gold?"

"Not since I was a kid. I think it was an overnight field trip to the 'Gold Country.' How about you? Where did you go?"

"Jamestown … in central California. Neal took me, and a buddy of his joined us. Although it was kind of a long drive from his place, we had a real blast … and I discovered gold!" Adam exclaimed as he pulled a little plastic bottle from his shirt pocket. "See?"

"Wow, you're rich," I said. The concept of panning for gold didn't especially excite me, but then I had done it fifteen years earlier on a field trip with two dozen other fifth-graders, so the moment was not as magical for me as it was for Adam.

"This trip has really helped me appreciate something," Adam said. "More than anything else, it's helped me understand how important it is for us to follow our heart. I wish I could travel all over the world. Besides California, I've always wanted to visit Hawaii."

I nodded my head.

"How about you, Will? Where in the world do you want to go?"

I contemplated for a minute. "Except for a family reunion in St. Louis when I was in junior high school, the closest I've been to the South has been a layover in New Orleans. Exploring that part of the country has held my interest as there is so much history there, and from what I hear, the people are very friendly."

"Don't believe everything you hear," said Adam as he leaned over and kissed my neck. "We can tell someone to go straight to hell, but by the time it comes out of a southerner's mouth, it sounds much nicer."

"You mean you choose your words more carefully?"

Adam shook his head. "Will, you always need to read between the lines. Sometimes what we're really saying lies somewhere between the words we speak and our inflection." He suggested I visit him in Memphis to discover the South with the help of a proper tour guide, especially since he was hosting a return to school party in August. Then I could explore a few of the treasured out-of-the-way spots that only a southerner could show me. Pointing out that had it not been for me, he would not have discovered Malibu and Laguna Beach, Adam's suggestion jarred me. I had never before known someone so interested in spending time with me. I explained that I didn't yet have my schedule for August, but Adam countered by saying it would mean a lot to him if I could make it to his party, which was celebrating the beginning of his final year of medical school. Pleading with me to visit, I agreed to bid for that time off.

South of the village in Laguna Beach, I turned off of Pacific Coast Highway and headed down a narrow street lined with old cottages and newly con-structed homes which provided commanding views of the ocean below us. "I'm taking you to one of my favorite spots in Laguna," I explained as I found a parking spot in front of the beach house owned by Ozzie and Harriet Nelson.

Adam followed close behind me as I led the way down a concrete staircase that brought us to a nearly secluded beach just as the sun was beginning its daily decline to the west. Surrounded by a wide variety of tide pools and little coves, which were sheltered below huge bluffs, I led Adam to a perch, high atop a rock, protected from the rising tide. As the sun dipped behind the Palos Ver-des Peninsula, the ocean surrounded us.

"I'd give anything to stay here with you," said Adam. "This is where I've always dreamed of being … sitting on a beach in California."

"Nobody is forcing you to leave," I said.

"Will, as much as I would love to stay, I simply can't. My family expects me to finish medical school, and it's not as easy as you might think."

"Trust me, Adam. Nothing about medical school sounds easy to me. But you could always transfer to UCLA. They have one of the best medical schools in the country."

Adam was reflective as he picked up a pebble and tossed it towards the crashing wave in the distance. "If only things were different."

While we watched the sunset, I realized he was right. If only he didn't live in Memphis. If only the rest of the world was okay with the two of us being attracted to one another. If only … The list went on. But in truth, all I really wanted was to spend time with someone who cared about me as a person, not someone who just wanted to sleep with me to give them a sense of accomplishment. I was more than an object. I was a caring and affectionate human being who wanted to explore the world … preferably with someone. And the more time I spent with Adam, I was beginning to think he could be that someone.

As the sun faded to the west, I kissed Adam in the twilight of the evening. By displaying affection with another man in public along the shore of the Pacific Ocean, I was breaking every Orange County moral rule. Yet somehow it didn't matter. Being together was all that seemed important.

Adam put his arm around me and leaned his head against my shoulder. Except for the crashing of the waves in the distance, the moment was perfectly serene. Adam's scent aroused me. His long, muscular body was perfectly proportioned and the hair that covered his chiseled chest gave him the appearance of a model. He was, at twenty-five years of age, the equivalent of a Greek god. I glanced down at his feet, covered in sand, and smiled. I realized my attraction for him went beyond the physical aspect, and I seized the moment and kissed him—a fraction of time that lasted for several minutes.

"Why does it feel so right being with you?" I asked.

Adam flashed a smile. "I don't know, Will, but I feel the same way as you do. I really could stay here forever … sitting next to you."

The sunset created an orange hue that lingered above the Palos Verdes peninsula, jutting out from the north. Nearly thirty miles across the Pacific, Catalina Island was visible on the horizon. I fantasized about spending a weekend with Adam. Just being with him for a couple of days would help prove if this feeling was more than a simple case of raging testosterone. Then I remembered his invitation for me to come to Memphis. Somehow the idea of spending time with Adam in a place more accepting than Orange County sounded like a great idea.

In the twilight, we left Victoria Beach and drove towards the village. Despite it being the Fourth of July weekend, I managed to find a parking space in front of the restaurant known simply as "The Place Across the Street From the Hotel Laguna." My exceptional luck at having good parking karma continued as we walked into the restaurant, which was packed with people waiting to be seated for dinner. The host cast us a knowing smile and immediately seated us at a table in the corner of the restaurant, providing us privacy yet affording us a great view of the restaurant.

I glanced up to find Adam studying the eclectic collection of art that surrounded the brick walls of the restaurant, featuring an assortment of seascapes, still life paintings, replicas of well-known works, and several plein air paintings. A portrait captured Adam's attention across the room featuring an elderly man with long grey hair and a straggly white beard dressed in overalls, wearing an old hat that was battered and torn. His arm was raised, almost as if he was waving at someone in the distance.

"That's an amazing painting," said Adam. "Who is that?"

I turned to discover what Adam was drawn to. "Oh, that's Eiler Larsen. He's the town greeter." Explaining that the Danish immigrant arrived in Laguna during the late thirties, he took up his volunteer post as the unofficial "greeter" of Laguna where he could usually be seen during the day waving as cars passed the intersection of Pacific Coast Highway and Forest Avenue. "I haven't seen him in a while, but he's kind of an eccentric character. My understanding is Mr. Larsen arrived here with little in his pockets, yet he has made Laguna Beach his home for over thirty years. What's really amazing is he never learned how to drive, but Mr. Larsen speaks six languages."

Adam was taken by the story. "I wish I could meet him. I wonder what his interests are … besides people?"

I reflected for a minute. "I've heard he loves books, especially the poetry of Louis Untemeyer, who is an American author and poet best known for a magazine he founded which introduced new poets, including Robert Frost."

"So you like poetry?" asked Adam.

"I find it fascinating. But then some people understand math formulas," I said, brushing my foot against Adam's leg.

Adam nodded his head.

"Not me," I said. "I like reading stories that rhyme."

While sharing appetizers, Adam admitted he was curious about what made Laguna so special. I explained that this little seaside village was the west coast's most famous year-round art colony. Each summer, several festivals were produced, the most renowned of which was the annual "Pageant of the Masters." For two months every summer, the Pageant played to sold-out audiences in an outdoor amphitheater, accompanied by an orchestra performing an original score with live narration, intricate sets and state-of-the-art lighting, presenting a ninety-minute theatrical recreation of classical and contemporary works of art with real people posing to look exactly like their counterparts in the original pieces. Adam was fascinated as I explained that Laguna was also a place where gay men found refuge because of the tolerant nature and bohemian lifestyle of many of the residents who made this seaside village their permanent home.

"You're very lucky to have discovered this beautiful spot," said Adam. "How far away do you live from here?"

"Newport Beach is the next town up the coast, but I grew up spending summers here in Laguna, so in many ways this feels like my home."

"Tell me what your summers were like."

"Well, they were pretty unique," I explained. "My days were spent at the beach, people-watching, surfing and just exploring the natural beauty of the tide pools and coves."

"You surf?" asked Adam.

"Practically every morning. You should come with me tomorrow and I'll teach you." I explained how surfing was my way of communing with nature that helped keep me grounded. "With all of the craziness of this world, when I'm in the water, riding a good wave, it's almost as if everything is in balance. I feel invincible when I'm on my board. It's the one place I can go and be surrounded by nothing bad."

Adam nodded his head. "I wish I had a place to go that made me feel safe from everything."

It surprised me that Adam would need a place to hideaway. For some reason, I presumed living in the South meant that nothing complicated ever happened. I imagined life to be free from pressure, unlike living in southern California. I envisioned Adam grew up surrounded by plantation homes with butlers and maids, and that his parents drank mint juleps on the porch every evening while children played outside. Living in the South was, I fantasized, quite simple, and the pleasures I had read about were probably part of one's everyday existence.

"Let me tell you something," Adam said as he lowered his head. "Since I graduated from college, my summers have been spent trying to avoid the pressure of medical school. And this past semester was especially rough for me … and my GPA slipped a little. My father told me I need to improve my grades, so I'm not looking forward to the next term. My counselor said, 'Adam, it's sink or swim.' I know it's going to be a tough year for me."

"I'm sure it's something you'll be able to achieve," I said. "Especially since it sounds like your father is so supportive of your career choice."

Adam glanced at the painting of Eilier Larsen. "I would hardly characterize him as supportive, Will. My going to medical school is his dream, not mine."

I listened as Adam explained that his father had been anything but supportive while he matriculated through college. When he decided to try out for the cheerleading squad, his father chided Adam for pursuing what was "something girls did." I understood completely what Adam was saying. When I decided to become a flight attendant, my father was less than overwhelmed. He traveled frequently on business and did not consider the job of a flight attendant as a man's career. My mother, on the other hand, was nothing but supportive. "Think of all of the exciting places you will explore, Will," was her reaction when I announced I had been accepted to the flight attendant training program. Exploring the world meant that I could expand my horizons, and my mother encouraged me to follow my dreams.

"Spending summers here must have been really special," Adam remarked.

While I reminisced upon my family's first summer in Laguna, Adam listened as I described our cottage on Sleepy Hollow Lane, a stone's throw from the beach. I explained how my dad traveled a lot on business, so he was home only on weekends. My mother was a schoolteacher, and even though she taught summer school, she was home every night to prepare dinner.

"You spent every day at the beach?" Adam asked enviously.

"My board and I were buddies," I explained. "Every morning I went surfing, and then I had lunch on the beach. Afterwards, I would surf for a couple more hours before returning home for dinner. As I think back, I realize my summers in Laguna were the best part of growing up." And it was true. Sunlight and laughter took me far away from the shadows of my mind.

Adam's smile helped me appreciate how special those summers were. And meeting him seemed to reinforce that summer was a time to explore new places, meet new people and expand one's horizons. While waiting for dinner, people coveted our table. We savored our starters, lingered over the entrees while enjoying a bottle of wine, and although we declined dessert, Adam and I were in no rush to leave the restaurant. We found something neither of us had discovered: a place to hide away where we could truly be ourselves ... far from the madness of the world.

CHAPTER 6

※

The hills and canyons situated between Laguna and Newport Beach were part of the expansive Irvine Ranch, an undeveloped strip of land along Pacific Coast Highway. During daylight hours, one could stop at the Irvine Ranch and rent a horse for a ride along the beach, something that made this stretch of beach north of Laguna like nowhere else in southern California. A favorite past time of mine was to stop for a peanut butter-banana-date shake at the Crystal Cove Shake Shack. I was convinced no one made a better shake. With the lights from the village twinkling behind us, the darkness of the night reminded me that Adam and I had spent twenty-four hours together.

"What is Memphis like?" I asked.

"It's so much fun," Adam said. "There are over a dozen colleges all over Memphis, so there is a party almost every night of the week. Besides being the home of Elvis and the birthplace of blues, there are college students every-where throughout the year. And we're surrounded by some very cool out of the way places to visit." Adam could have worked for the Chamber of Commerce. The more he talked about all of the fun things to do there, I believed a visit to Memphis would be an unforgettable experience.

The lights from Corona del Mar—an unincorporated portion of Newport Beach where I lived—appeared in the distance and I glanced towards Adam to find him looking at me. "We're almost home," I said as I moved my hand onto his leg.

Nodding his head, I realized I was unprepared for his visit. When I left for Studio One on Friday night, I did not anticipate having a houseguest twenty-four hours later. My mind began to do a summersault as I feared how messy my apartment might be. Not that my place was unkempt, but I wanted in the worst way to make a good impression, and I did not want Adam to discover my bad traits right off the bat. Leaving my apartment in less than good order was one of them.

"When we get to your apartment, can we take a bubble bath?" asked Adam as he touched my hand resting on his thigh.

I hadn't taken a bubble bath since I was a kid. I wasn't even sure I had the right soap. And even more disconcerting was I was pretty sure my bathtub was far from clean. The possibilities of making a negative impression caused my head to spin, but Adam eased my concerns when he leaned over and kissed my neck.

Walking into my apartment, I was relieved to discover the dishes from dinner on Friday night were in the dishwasher and the kitchen was clean. Glancing around my apartment, I remembered my laundry was all done for my upcoming trip. Relieved that I didn't have to focus on the mundane things a flight attendant must deal with on their days off, I noticed Adam glancing through a notebook on the coffee table, containing a collection of short stories I had written in college accompanied by photos I had taken from the various places I had visited while growing up.

"You wrote this?" he asked.

I nodded my head.

"How long did it take you?"

"It's a collection of travel stories I wrote over a couple of summers while I was in college. I submitted it as a senior project, and my professor blew me away when he said he really liked it."

"That's very cool. Are you going to get it published?"

"He said I should submit it. But I haven't pursued anything yet."

"Why not?" asked Adam.

"I don't know. They're just stories about stuff that was in my head growing up. I'm a little embarrassed about it."

"Wow, Will, I'm very impressed. You shouldn't be embarrassed. I wish I could write."

"Doctors write more than authors," I said. "They write in medical charts, they write prescriptions, doctor's orders and what else? Oh, all of those medical journals they write."

"How do you know about all of that stuff?"

My face went blank. "I've been to the doctor a few times. My first thought is always the same thing. No one can read their handwriting."

Adam laughed. "Will, I've never heard anyone put it in that perspective. You're pretty observant."

I shrugged my shoulders. "Do you want to see upstairs?"

Adam nodded his head.

I took him by the hand through the dining area and led him up the stairs to the bedroom where we kissed … for a real long time.

❦   ❦   ❦

"What kind of medicine do you want to practice?" I asked Adam while I massaged his shoulders.

"I'm considering pediatrics. During the rotation we had last term, I enjoyed spending time with kids the most. They are so vulnerable and impressionable, yet they are the most honest patients we studied all year long. Treating children is really much easier than adults," Adam said as he moved his foot across the base of the tub, starting a conga line with the bubbles from the bath.

"We need more doctors who are compassionate," I said as I kissed the back of his neck. "When I was growing up, I had chronic ear aches and my parents searched for quite a while to find someone who could treat me."

"How long ago was this?"

"I was five."

"Treating ears, nose and throats has come a long way since then. But it's still a tough specialty."

"My parents first took me to a general practitioner who found an accumulation of ear wax. He recommended puncturing my ear drum to drain the fluid."

"Ouch. You must have been scared."

"Oh, my God, are you kidding? I was petrified."

"Did he perform the procedure?"

"Yep … with the help of Nurse Ratchet, who held me down when I saw the doctor enter the examining room with a needle that was longer than my arm. My parents had to peel me off the ceiling afterwards."

"Did you have your tonsils removed?"

"Eventually. After another visit to the ear drum poker, when I began to scream hysterically, my father put his foot down and said, 'Enough. You're not going to do that to my son again.' My parents found a specialist—I forgot what kind of doctor he was—"

"—An otolaryngologist?"

"Is that an ENT doctor?"

"Yes."

"Adam, this guy was really cool and he was so gentle with me. During my first visit with him he explained he needed to do a tonsillectomy and showed me a plastic model of the inner ear so I understood what was happening to my body."

"How did you tolerate the surgery?"

"Like a little soldier."

"Have you considered having a myringotomy?"

"Fortunately, my ear problems vanished."

"You're really lucky that you're able to fly. You could have had permanent ear damage from the first doctor, who sounds like he may have overstepped his area of expertise."

"I was really nervous when I went for my physical at Continental, but the company doctor checked me out and I passed the physical and the hearing test with flying colors."

"Will, your parents were very brave to do what they did. Back then, to defy a doctor was tantamount to breaking the law. Your father is a courageous man for taking you to another doctor."

I held Adam in my arms as I thought about that frightful experience. "I've repressed so much of that time of my life from my mind. Talking about it now helps me realize how frightened I was."

"It must have been a terrifying experience to go through, especially at such a young age."

"I think it scarred me for life with doctors."

Adam rubbed his hands along my thighs. "I promise I'll never hurt you."

❦   ❦   ❦

In the early light of daybreak on Sunday, I opened my eyes to find Adam smiling at me. "What?" I asked.

"You have the look of someone who is very content with life," said Adam as he kissed me.

How could I be anything but content? My mother, calling to invite me to dinner, interrupted our kiss. "You can leave from here and go straight to the airport," she said when I demurred her invitation.

I explained that a friend was visiting from out of town and he and I were going to spend the day together before heading up to the airport. Despite her gentle persuasiveness to bring Adam with me to dinner, I was resolute in declining her spontaneous invitation.

"But Will, I want you to meet our new neighbors. You will really like them."

"They've just moved in, Mom. I'll meet them next time."

Adam was glancing through a collection of photos I took when I had visited Hawaii earlier in the year. I climbed back into bed and kissed him.

"Where do your parents live?" he asked.

"In a little seaside colony near Long Beach, about thirty minutes away. For the past year, my parents have been enduring construction while a new house was built next to their home. Living at the beach has its privileges, but the trade off for a phenomenal ocean view is often times you can hear your neighbors sneeze."

Adam laughed. "I guess it's a good thing I'm not too loud when I'm having sex."

"You're perfect," I said, wrapping my arms around him. "I wouldn't change a thing about you."

"Even if I can't surf?"

"I'm about to change that!"

❧   ❧   ❧

After securing my six foot eight inch Bruce Jones retro swallow winger surfboard in the back of my truck, I drove us to the storage locker behind the apartment complex where I kept my backup surfboard, a seven foot "egg" that was perfect for Adam. Having used it after storms when the surf tended to be more violent, it provided lots of flotation and good maneuverability, even in rough waves.

We drove to Crystal Cove, north of Laguna, where there was a steady swell of about four feet, ideal conditions for Adam's surfing debut. Grabbing our boards, I explained the basics about surfing as I led Adam down a path below the parking area towards the beach.

Adam had a clear advantage over most beginners by being a good swimmer. After we waxed our boards, we waded into the water until we were thigh-deep. Then I held Adam's board as he sat on it to give him a little familiarity. Grabbing my board, I hopped on and paddled alongside Adam. Together we headed out and began to play with our boards. Adam was a natural as he rolled onto his board, flipping it over and righting it with his body evenly distributed. He got the basics of handling the board wired in only a few minutes. Next I showed Adam the more difficult techniques: turning, rolling and duck diving, and before he knew it, Adam was ready for his first attempt at surfing.

"How am I doing?" he asked, grinning from ear to ear.

"You have the dexterity of a kid," I said as Adam paddled towards me. "You're a natural, and you have an unbelievable sense of balance. It took me an entire day to do what you've accomplished in under an hour."

Having agility helped pave the "wave" for Adam, but developing the technique of surfing is something that takes a long time to acquire, no matter how skilled you may be. Adam's patience was what made our first day in the water so much fun. Despite his valiant efforts, he never made it on the board to connect with a wave, but he did manage to stand up several times, which was more than I did the first day I learned how to surf.

Perhaps what made teaching Adam seem effortless was his laughter, which was contagious. Every time he fell off his board, he would belly flop into the water, coming up to the surface with a huge grin before spitting water from his mouth.

"Now I know what a fish must feel like," he said after nearly two hours of courageous attempts to ride a wave.

"Fish don't surf," I replied.

"Neither do I," he said, grinning.

🍁   🍁   🍁

After stopping for brunch at Coco's Restaurant in the village of Corona del Mar, Adam asked me where I went to clear my head.

"I'll show you," I said. Walking along Pacific Coast Highway, I explained how Corona del Mar had named its streets after plants, flowers and trees, alphabetically from A through P. We walked a few blocks to Goldenrod Avenue where I led us through a neighborhood of well-manicured lawns and modest bungalow-style homes to the end of the street. Next, we crossed a footbridge connecting the village to a bluff overlooking Little Poppy Beach beyond the parkway, at the end of Newport Harbor. The Pacific Ocean expanded the horizon for as far as we could see.

Walking along the rocks that lined the bluff and protected the mouth of the harbor from erosion, I found a spot for us to watch the boats traveling in and out of Newport Harbor. "This is where I watch the sunset almost every night that I'm in town."

Adam was taken by the view. "This is unbelievable. The beaches in California just seem to keep getting better."

While Adam watched the boats, I reflected upon him trying to ride a wave. "You did really well today."

Adam shook his head. "I wish I could stay and work on my balance."

"What time do you fly back to Memphis?"

"My flight leaves at ten o'clock. How about you, Will? When do you fly out again?"

"Just after midnight."

"Where to?"

"It's a four-day trip. Tonight I fly to Houston. Tomorrow morning I work a flight to Miami. Then on to Las Vegas on Tuesday and Chicago on Wednesday before returning home Thursday morning."

"God, I wish I could go with you."

"So do I, Adam. Nothing would make me happier than to have you with me."

We enjoyed the quiet of the moment, watching boats come and go from the Newport marina, gazing out at the Pacific Ocean. Not wanting the moment to end, I leaned over and kissed Adam. It didn't matter that I was in conservative Orange County and that every Republican that owned a house overlooking the ocean or a boat cruising on the bay could see us. All that mattered was this moment, which I did not want to end.

After we kissed, Adam reclined against the rocks. "Will, this visit has really been great for me. I have totally mellowed out. You've made me realize how important it is to have fun. Medical school is so competitive and vigorous, and if that isn't enough, there is the pressure from my father to do well. I didn't realize it, but all that expectation has really taken a toll on me."

I listened as Adam explained that medical school was far different than college. It was pass or fail with no in between. As I watched him, I felt as if I had known him all of my life.

"What are you thinking?" he asked.

"I'm having a hard time believing that we just met."

"Why?"

"Because I feel like I've known you forever."

"Maybe we knew each other in a different lifetime?"

❀   ❀   ❀

While walking through the TWA concourse at LAX, the hallowed walls of the terminal echoed our footsteps as we both avoided the inevitable farewell.

"Adam, I'm not very good at good-byes," I said. "I so wish things were different …"

Adam smiled and held a finger over my mouth. "Things will be different, Will. You are going to visit me next month. Memphis will never be the same again." He pulled out a little bottle from his shirt pocket and handed it to me.

"What's this?" I asked.

"Gold. I panned for it the second day I was here. All I wanted to do was come to California and discover gold. And I found it," he said as he placed the bottle in my shirt pocket.

"What are you doing?"

"It's something to guarantee you'll come visit me next month."

I stood there in disbelief as Adam wrapped his arms around me and hugged me.

❀   ❀   ❀

Watching Adam's jet push back from the jet way, I realized my wish may have come true. I had finally discovered someone to explore the world with. As I watched the TWA jet taxi towards the runway, I remembered the lyric Jane Olivor sang from "Some Enchanted Evening" at "The Back Lot" a few weeks earlier. *Once you have found him, never let him go.*

CHAPTER 7

As passengers boarded Continental flight number fifty, the "red-eye" to Miami, with an intermediate stop at Houston's Intercontinental Airport, all I could think about was Adam. Reminiscing upon the two days we spent together was like watching a movie in my mind. As people filed by me, searching for their seats, I was far, far away. I could still smell his fragrance, and just thinking about his body close to mine began to arouse me. By now his flight was half way to Memphis, and I wondered if Adam was thinking about me.

"Can I hang my garment bag here?" asked a passenger as I gazed beyond the first class cabin.

"Sure," I replied, distracted by his interrupting the movie in my mind.

"Thanks," he said. "Are you working in first class?"

I nodded my head and then realized I needed to focus on work.

"Would it be too much to ask if I could move to a window seat? I hope to catch some sleep during the flight and don't want to have someone crawling over me to use the restroom."

I glanced at him. A nice-looking guy in his thirties, with far too much energy for a Sunday at midnight, meant he was in need of some attention. Usually men traveling alone gravitated towards Helen, the first flight attendant, but this guy appeared oblivious that any other crew member was on board besides me. "We only have four passengers booked in first class," I said. "So you can sit anywhere you would like once everyone has boarded."

The man smiled and nodded his head. "That's why I like this airline. You guys are always so accommodating. I used to fly Delta, and their flight attendants always say they are happy that you're aboard, then they disappear and you can never get a drink."

"Speaking of something to drink, may I bring you anything before we push back?" I asked.

"See, that's what I mean," the man replied. "I'm Peter, by the way."

"Hi Peter. I'm Will. It's nice to have you on board tonight."

"How about a gin and tonic?"

"Coming right up," I said.

"With a lime."

As I mixed Peter's drink, I glanced at Helen. "He's all yours," she said, shaking her head. Helen and I had flown this trip the month before and were quite accustomed to first class passengers who needed attention. Most people flying at this hour had to get to Houston by the next morning for a meeting, a funeral or to spend time with a dying relative. The rest of the pack took the overnight flight to save money. Fares on late night flights were heavily discounted since the aircraft was being positioned for a morning departure, and the significant payload was cargo. So carrying revenue passengers became pure profit for Continental. Normally, a Sunday night would have been booked at sixty percent capacity, but because tomorrow was the Fourth of July, the load factor was less than forty percent, which meant the cabin crew would have plenty of time to read, work on crossword puzzles, or, like I was intending to do, plan their next vacation.

I placed Peter's drink, a couple of bags of peanuts and a cocktail napkin on a serving tray as an off-duty Continental pilot, his wife and twelve-year-old son boarded the Boeing seven-twenty-seven jet.

"Good evening, Will," said the pilot. "How are you doing tonight?"

"Hey, Captain. Are you heading back to Houston?"

"Yeah, we're heading home after spending the weekend with my parents. They had quite a celebration up in Malibu."

"You guys are welcome to sit wherever you would like," I said as I delivered Peter's drink. "We're only booked with four passengers up here."

"How was your weekend?" asked the Captain.

"It was really nice," I said, grinning from ear to ear. "A friend of mine was visiting from Memphis, and I took him to the beach yesterday. This morning we went surfing. It was so incredibly beautiful and the waves were perfect." It felt good to talk about Adam, and as I reflected upon our brief time together, I realized how present he was in my life.

"Where did you go surfing?" asked Peter as he moved from the window seat back to the aisle seat.

"Laguna Beach."

"That's so funny. I live in Laguna."

"What a small world."

"What beach do you surf at?"

"It varies from day to day."

"I like West Street Beach the best."

I nodded my head. West Street was the most popular beach amongst gay men, but the waves there never materialized to anything, so it was not a great surfing spot.

"Maybe we could go surfing together some time?" he suggested.

I shot Peter a look that established a boundary and conveyed that I was not interested. "Because of my schedule, I tend to be pretty spontaneous and don't make plans. It just sort of happens. And I surf a lot in Newport and Seal Beach, too."

While the Captain and his family were getting settled, I offered them something to drink. Helen made the flight verification announcement, indicating we were about to push back. The image of Adam's handsome face flashed in my mind. While I was in the galley making their drinks, Helen glanced at me. "Will, you're distracted. What's going on?"

"Nothing," I replied. "I'm still thinking about the beach," although the grin on my face told her I was reflecting on more than the fact it had been a great beach day.

❧   ❧   ❧

"I think you should call him when we get to the hotel," Helen suggested as we secured our shoulder restraints and seat belts while the jet descended over Houston.

"You don't think it would be too pushy?"

"Will, look at it this way. If you don't call, he won't know you're thinking about him. As my mother always says, 'Out of sight means out of mind.'"

"But I'm not much of a caller …"

Helen straightened her skirt and checked her nylons for any sign of a run. "I think you need to ask yourself if he's someone you want to get to know better. And if he is, what's the harm in giving him a call? It would please your mother to no end. I can just imagine her reaction when she discovers her son, a nice Jewish boy, is dating a doctor."

My mind began to race as Helen's comment changed my perspective on things. Adam and I had never discussed religion. What if he was a neo-Nazi?

❧   ❧   ❧

After getting out of my uniform, I took a quick shower to remove all of the "Boeing essence" from my body before putting on a clean T-shirt and pair of boxers. Sitting on the edge of the bed, I looked at the piece of paper I carried in my uniform shirt pocket with Adam's phone number on it and contemplated whether or not to call him.

My hand was trembling as I dialed his number from the telephone in my hotel room. To my relief, I got a busy signal.

After a few minutes, I tried the number again. After one ring, a familiar voice answered.

"Hello?"

"Adam, how are you?"

"Will?"

"Yeah, it's me."

"I can't believe you're calling me. I just spoke with your supervisor in California."

"But I'm in Miami."

"I know. I called the flight attendant office in Los Angeles and they told me you were on a trip."

"You called Continental?"

"Yeah. I knew you were gone for a few days, but I really wanted to talk to you. I didn't know how else to get in touch with you."

As I listened, my hand stopped shaking.

"Will, I had such a great time in California, thanks to you, and I know you're going to try and visit me next month … but I can't wait 'til then to see you again. I want you to visit as soon as you can."

I didn't know what to say. I wanted to see Adam, too, but I couldn't bring myself to tell him how I felt.

"August is three weeks away. Will, is there any way you can get here sooner?"

"Adam, I don't know what to say. I—"

"—You don't have to say anything, Will. Just get here, okay? I really want to spend some more time with you … and there's someone I want you to meet."

"Who?" I asked.

"Damien."

"Who's Damien?"

"He's my new roommate ... and until you get here, he spends every night with me."

I felt nauseous. Adam was sleeping with his roommate.

"Will, it's not what you think. Some friends of mine got me a puppy to keep me company. I've named him Damien."

Relieved that he and his roommate were platonic, I took a deep breath and exhaled. "What kind of puppy is he?" I managed to ask, disguising my fragile mental state.

"He's an Afghan. And he's really looking forward to meeting you."

"Well, I get back to L.A. on Thursday morning."

"Can we spend the weekend together? Please, Will ... it would mean so much to me ... especially since I return to school in a couple of weeks."

"Let me see what I can do."

Helen called in a favor with the manager of Continental's Pass Bureau, and I was issued an interline pass on American Airlines in less than twenty-four hours. Normally, it would have taken three business days to obtain a pass on another airline, but since Adam was adamant about seeing me that weekend, Helen felt it was necessary to intervene. "You need to go," she said in her maternal way as we checked in for our flight to Chicago Wednesday afternoon. "And when I see you on Sunday night, I expect a full report."

I was surprised at how green Tennessee was from thirty thousand feet. The Smokey Mountains framed the surrounding communities in a way similar to the Lake District along the English countryside. Throughout the four-hour flight, the American Airlines flight attendants treated me like I was part of their family. Providing me with suggestions of where to sample the signature Memphis culinary staple, barbequed anything, I was euphoric as the jet descended. Teasing me about having never been to the birthplace of soul music and the home of Elvis, the first class flight attendant presented me with a bottle of champagne to help celebrate my arrival.

Adam was waiting for me at the end of the jet way door. Dressed in a beige polo shirt and off-white cut-off shorts, his dark complexion radiated against his bright smile. He gave me a huge hug and kiss as I entered the terminal. We may have embraced longer than we should have as I noticed a few people looking at us when Adam planted another kiss on my neck. "You look much better than I remember," he said grabbing my overnight bag.

As we walked through the terminal, I couldn't stop smiling. Adam kept glancing at me, shaking his head in disbelief, flashing his infectious smile. "I can't believe you're here."

Neither could I. For the first time since working for Continental, I had done something completely spontaneous. Returning to California as the morning sun was beginning to burn through the Los Angeles haze, I bolted from Continental's terminal to stand by for American's noon-time non-stop flight to Memphis. Without blinking an eye, I was on my way to a new destination without any plan other than to spend time with someone I barely knew. My sense of adventure had overtaken me. To my surprise, I was not afraid of the unknown. Never before had I just gotten on an airplane and flown somewhere without a plan … yet I felt so comfortable being with Adam that it seemed perfectly natural to spend a couple more days with him, albeit two thousand miles from home.

The familiarity of being near him diminished whatever concerns I should have had. While on layovers, many of my co-workers did what I was doing—get to know someone better—the difference was they had an agenda. My only desire was to truly get to know Adam better. Yet, as we approached the parking lot, I realized how little I knew about him. We stopped as Adam opened the trunk of a Buick Riviera and tossed my overnight bag in. I had not even imagined what type of car he would have. Not that it mattered, but that was the sort of thing that revealed a little bit about someone. "So this is what doctors drive these days?" I asked.

"It's what *I* drive," Adam replied confidently as he opened the passenger door for me. It was actually Adam's roommate's car that he had borrowed to pick me up.

I reached into my shirt pocket for a small plastic bottle. "I brought something for you," I said as Adam climbed into the front seat.

Leaning towards me, he kissed my neck and brushed his hand through my long hair. "All I wanted was for you to get here. You have no idea how happy I am."

Smiling, I handed the little plastic bottle to Adam. "I brought a little bit of California with me," I said.

"What's this?" he asked.

"It's the gold you found when you were in California last week."

❦   ❦   ❦

"You should have the catfish," Adam said as I studied the menu. "It's out of this world." The aroma from the kitchen aroused my stomach. As I sipped my freshly brewed iced tea, flavored with mint and lemon, Adam nudged my leg with his foot. Looking up, his wide grin distracted me.

"You boys ready to order?" asked the waitress.

"He needs a couple of minutes," Adam said.

"Take your time, honey," the waitress said as she stuck her pencil into the mound of hair piled on top of her head and returned the order pad to the pocket of her freshly starched uniform. "More tea?" she asked as Adam nodded his head.

"Is everyone this friendly?" I asked.

"Remember, Will. Don't believe everything you hear. We can tell someone to go straight to hell, but by the time it comes out of a southerner's mouth, it sounds much nicer."

Nodding my head, I looked around the restaurant. It was as if time had stopped. No one appeared to be in a hurry. The ceiling fans were the only things moving faster than a snail's pace, circulating the thick, humid air that hung overhead. I wondered if the humidity was the reason people were nearly catatonic. Even the bus boy clearing a table across from us seemed unmotivated by the line of people waiting to be seated. I watched as he reached across the table, extending his muscular black arm to wipe the table clean. Glancing towards the entrance, I was mesmerized by the collection of memorabilia that adorned the walls.

"You're fascinating to watch," said Adam.

"I am?"

"You study everything. I'll bet you read a lot."

I was taken by Adam's observation. "It just feels so different being here."

"You'll see how life is really not that much different than in California. We just put on a better show."

When the waitress returned, I followed Adam's recommendation and ordered the catfish with hushpuppies and purple hull peas.

"Would you like biscuits or cornbread?" asked the waitress.

"Cornbread," Adam volunteered.

CHAPTER 8

The faint ringing of a telephone awakened me. In the back of my mind, I feared it was Continental crew scheduling calling to reassign my trip. As I opened my eyes, Adam's smile greeted me. "Good morning, sunshine" he said, brushing his hand through my hair.

"Hey," I replied, relieved that I was only dreaming about being on a layover.

Adam's roommate knocked gently on the bedroom door. "Adam, Jim is on the phone. He and Bob are going to the river and want to know if you and Will want to join them."

Adam leaned down and kissed me. "Want to spend the day at the beach?" he asked.

I nodded my head.

"Ask him to pick us up in an hour," Adam said as I buried my head against his stomach.

"I'm nervous about meeting your friends," I said reluctantly.

"Don't be," Adam replied, reassuringly. "They think you're a celebrity, coming all the way from California just to visit me."

An hour later we were on our way to the "the beach" (along side the Mississippi River), basking in the sun that drenched Jim's convertible. I glanced at the cooler wedged in between the two front bucket seats, which contained a fifth of vodka, Bloody Mary mix, plastic container with sliced limes, olives and celery sticks, and a bottle of hot sauce. As Jim headed onto the expressway, Bob poured each of us a drink as I watched in disbelief. We were about to consume alcoholic beverages while driving. Apparently, in Tennessee it didn't matter.

"Adam tells us you're a flight attendant," said Bob, handing me a Bloody Mary.

"Yes," I said as Adam put his arm around my shoulders.

"Some people work with a full galley," said Jim, glancing at me through the rear view mirror. "We just have a mini-bar." He lifted up his cup and toasted me. "Cheers."

I raised my plastic cup and smiled. "Thanks for inviting me to join you guys."

"It must be so exciting flying all over the world," said Bob.

"I don't fly across the continent," I confessed. "At least not yet. But I'm enjoying seeing parts of the country I didn't even know existed."

"How long have you been flying?" asked Jim, who seemed more interested in looking at us through the rear view mirror than focusing on the Interstate.

"Only a couple of months."

As we crossed the state line and entered Arkansas, Adam explained how growing up in the South produced his early images of "the beach," which was a long, flat stretch of muddy clay that surrounded the edge of the Mississippi River. "Of course that all changed when I met you," he said. "I still can't believe I was there last week. Did I tell you guys Will taught me how to surf?"

"Yes," said Bob, sipping his Bloody Mary. "You've mentioned it every day since you returned from California."

Adam closed his eyes as the wind provided a momentary respite from the hot, sticky August morning. "I can still feel the sensation of being on the waves."

"You sure that's from riding a wave?" asked Jim, raising his eyebrows.

"I went to Hawaii a couple of years ago," Bob said. "Are the beaches in California similar?"

"Not really," I said. "California beaches pale by comparison. Hawaii is so much more lush and tropical. Just like in the film 'South Pacific'—except I don't think there's any gold there."

"Speaking of gold, look what I found when I first got there," said Adam.

"Oh my," said Bob as he studied the little plastic bottle Adam proudly displayed before handing it to Jim, who glanced at it while driving along the Interstate, swerving into the adjacent lane. I was becoming concerned we might not make it to the river with Jim's inattentive driving, but both Bob and Adam were nonplussed. I took another sip of my Bloody Mary and closed my eyes, taking comfort in my hope that the open container law was not enforced in the South.

"Can we go to Hawaii sometime?" asked Adam, rubbing my leg.

"Of course. Anytime you want to go," I promised, "we will go," even though I feared a head-on collision would prevent us from making it to "the beach."

"Maybe for Christmas?"

❦   ❦   ❦

"There's something I've been meaning to tell you," I said as we floated down the Mississippi River in two inner tubes.

"Please don't tell me you've been hiding a girlfriend. Or even worse, that you're married."

"No," I said, relieved that the several drinks we had consumed didn't impair Adam's sense of humor.

"I'm all ears."

"I don't celebrate Christmas."

"What? Why not?"

"'Cause I'm Jewish."

Adam smiled. "You must have been a little apprehensive about visiting me. Everyone here is either a born-again Christian or a Baptist."

"I admit I was a little nervous."

"Trust me. We're all relatively harmless. But I hope that doesn't change anything between us."

I reached toward Adam and held his hand as our inner tubes bobbed along the river. "Not at all," I replied. Floating along the river was a much different experience for me since there was no current and the expanse of water was far wider than any swimming pool I had ever been in.

As we drifted along the river, I confided about my less than traditional upbringing. "I have always been a dreamer," I said. "As a child, I followed visions of my own. While other kids were playing softball after school, I hung out in my tree house … inventing stories of my own. Then, when the rage was football, I took up surfing. Sometimes I think I was born to belong to the lines of a song. So often there's a sense of familiarity that makes me feel less vulnerable when I'm listening to music, and more often than not I've taken comfort in the lyric of a song."

Adam explained that he, too, was somewhat of a wandering soul. "Growing up was different for me as well. My father is in the Army, so we lived wherever he was stationed. It was sometimes hard to make friends in foreign countries, especially when I didn't know how long we would be living there."

"Where else have you lived?"

"For a while, my father was based in Japan. And for a couple of years, we were in Germany. But my family has lived in Dickson—near Nashville—for eight years. I went to high school in Japan, but graduated in Dickson."

"It must have been hard leaving behind friends in all of those other places."

"Being an Army brat, I don't believe in happy endings. But, for as rare as they are, Will, like a bright falling star, I think I may have found one in you."

My heart fluttered. "Really?"

"Yeah. Often my imagination has me reaching out too far," he said, keeping a firm hold on my inner tube. "But you knew who I was from the very start."

"Remember when we were at Little Poppy Beach last Sunday, when I told you I felt like I've known you forever?"

"Yes."

"What did you mean when you said maybe we knew each other in a different lifetime?"

Adam reflected. "I don't think I meant anything in particular. But I do feel like we've known each other for much longer than a week."

We continued to float along the river surrounded only by the serenading of birds and the trees rustling in the wind.

"Maybe I remind you of someone you knew growing up?"

Adam shook his head. "You are far too special to remind me of anyone else, Will."

I was so taken by his words. Despite the fact I was so far from home, being with Adam seemed perfectly natural. I was light-headed just being near him.

"Do you ever think about your plane crashing?" asked Adam.

I opened my eyes to the blazing sun directly overhead. "No," I replied, covering my eyes with my hand.

"You're not afraid?" asked Adam.

"No. Should I be?"

"It's just such a risky business. All those take-offs and landings. I would be a little nervous."

"I don't even think about it."

"What makes you so confident?"

"In truth, it comes from knowing that I've met someone unlike anyone else: you. And, if anything was to go wrong, I have you to save my day. After all, you're going to be a doctor, and doctors fix everything."

❧   ❧   ❧

After spending several hours in the water, and drinking one Bloody Mary too many, I took advantage of the seclusion of the landing we had discovered and kissed Adam. "I want to know everything about you," I said as we removed our swim trunks.

In the warmth of the afternoon sun, our lovemaking was unhurried. Adam allowed me to discover places I had never been before. Beyond the physical arousal of being alongside his chiseled torso, my excitement was heightened by the fact that we were surrounded by such natural beauty while making love along the Mississippi River. I was unconcerned that Bob and Jim might hear us. All that I cared about was discovering everything I could about Adam. I wanted to learn all about his past, and become a significant part of his future.

Holding me in his arms, I felt Adam's heart beating and realized how lucky we were to have found one another. After passionately kissing for nearly an hour, Adam turned on his side, facing me. "Do your parents know?" he asked, matter-of-factly.

"Yeah. They confronted me a while back. But I think they've always known. Especially my mom. Mothers have a way of knowing. It's their intuitive nature."

"How did they confront you?"

"I had stopped by for dinner one night. My mom gave me a look while she was setting the table and asked if I was seeing anyone. Just the way she asked the question made me realize she knew."

Adam nodded his head. "How is it mothers are so intuitive?"

"I don't know. But both of my parents have a sixth sense. My father has a sense of humor, and I am convinced my mother is clairvoyant. That night, as she served our dinner, she began to tell me a story about a teacher friend of hers from Ohio. He lived in Laguna Beach and taught art at my mom's school."

"He's gay," said Adam with an air of confidence.

"Yeah. And everyone knew it … except his parents, or so the story goes."

"So what happened?"

"One morning he didn't show up at school. And the principal's secretary knew the teacher and my mom were friends. So she called my mother to see if she could reach someone to check on this guy to make sure he was okay. My mom knew the teacher's landlord and contacted her. Long story short, the teacher was in his apartment and didn't appear to be alive. Once the paramedics arrived, they declared him dead. After the autopsy, his parents learned that he had died from a brain hemorrhage."

"And this was how your parents confronted you about being gay?"

"Yeah, it is. My mom explained how hard it was to watch her friend's parents react as they discovered his lifestyle when they arrived from Ohio to make burial arrangements and pack up his personal effects. My mother said it was heart wrenching when the teacher's mother discovered her son was gay."

"So she had no clue?"

"Apparently not. And my father asked if there was anything I wanted them to know as they didn't want to learn about my sexual preference in the same way this teacher's family did."

"Wow," said Adam. "Your parents are pretty cool and sound like they are very accepting."

"They are, in some ways, slightly ahead of their time."

"You're very fortunate, Will," Adam said as he leaned over and kissed my neck.

"How 'bout you?" I asked.

"We've never discussed it, but my father has made it very clear that my lifestyle must conform to his way of thinking."

"And what is his thinking?"

Adam looked away. "He told me before I left for California that queers have no place in society."

I was speechless. "You're kidding me."

"I wish I was. He would kill me if he knew I was interested in guys."

I couldn't believe what I was hearing. I realized that in many ways, living in the South was like living in a foreign country.

"And the pressure to become a doctor has sort of overwhelmed me," Adam said as he pulled my body closer. "I don't think I will ever live up to his expectations."

I reflected about my own father, who traveled nearly two weeks out of every month. I barely knew who he was. In some ways, he was a stranger who slept in the same house as me. Yet, I was in awe of him, and yearned to know who he really was. On Sunday afternoons, my father would go for a long walk along the beach. I always wondered what he was thinking, that stranger on the shore.

When my parents attended my graduation ceremony from Continental's flight training academy, I noticed for the first time in my life how proud my father was. "I don't know that anyone fulfills what their parent's expectations might be," I said. "After all, parents always want what they didn't have, or weren't able to achieve. There's nothing wrong with pursuing what *you* want, Adam, because, at the end of the day, only you can make yourself happy. Not your father … or anyone else."

"I wish it were as easy as just doing what I want to do, Will. But my whole career was planned out when I was sixteen. My father pushed me into the ROTC and everything was part of this big master plan. Now, unfortunately, I can't go back and undo three years of medical school."

"You can't tell your father that you don't want to be a doctor?"

Adam looked away. "That's just not something I can do. I live in constant fear of what will happen if I don't fulfill his expectations. He would kill me if I didn't follow through with this. When you join the Army, you're committed. Quitting is not an option."

"You're not quitting if you realize that being a doctor isn't what you want to do and go after whatever it is that you want. For one thing, aren't we supposed to do what makes us happy in life? How sad would that be to go through your whole life in a career you weren't interested in? Adam, you have to follow your dreams. At least that's what my German teacher always told me."

"It's easy for you, Will, because you're doing what you want to do."

"Trust me, Adam, I'm not going to fly forever. What I *really* want is to become a writer, but I have to experience life first."

"Maybe we could trade places?"

"What's the worst thing that would happen to you if you didn't finish medical school? Your father would eventually realize how important it is for you to do what makes you happy."

"It's hard for me to explain, but you need to understand my father's expectation for me to become a doctor is much greater than whatever it is I want to do with my life."

"But this isn't your father's life, Adam. It's *your* life."

Adam sighed. "If only things were different."

"You shouldn't think about it," I said as I kissed him. "At least not right now." Our tongues locked again and we made love once more.

Following our afternoon at the river, Jim drove to the Share Cropper, a restaurant in a shanty next to a train station in West Memphis, where Little Laura, a very large black woman, belted out show tunes from a small stage near the bar.

"This is like a supper club," I said as we found an empty table near the stage.

"We love coming here," said Jim as he waved to the singer. Blowing him a kiss, she continued to sing "I'm Going To Wash That Man Right Out Of My Hair."

After ordering drinks, Adam whispered in my ear. "Is there anything you want her to sing? She does songs on request."

I shook my head. Sitting next to Adam on the edge of Memphis was enough of a treat for me.

"She knows every ballad from practically every Broadway show," Bob explained. "This is where we take all of our friends from out of town."

As the song concluded, applause gathered strength from the tables near the bar. I followed Adam's lead as I put my hands together.

"Thank you, darlings," the owner said, glancing at our table. "Who is your good-looking friend?"

Adam smiled and put his arm around my shoulders. "This is Will. He's from California. Please sing him something to make him feel right at home."

"Coming right up, honey," she replied as she winked at me. "Welcome to the Share Cropper, Will."

As our drinks were being poured at the bar, we were treated to a very different rendition of "I Left My Heart In San Francisco." I was enchanted, and felt right at home. I was falling in love with Adam.

On Sunday morning, I discovered just how slow the pace was in the South. Adam took me food shopping at the Piggly Wiggly Market, America's first true self-service grocery store. Founded in Memphis by Clarence Saunders, grocery stores in the early twentieth century required shoppers to present their orders to clerks who gathered the goods from the store shelves. Saunders, a flamboyant and innovative man, noticed this method resulted in wasted time and man hours, so he came up with an unheard of solution that would revolutionize the entire grocery industry: he developed a way for shoppers to serve themselves.

While pushing a carriage through the store, I followed Adam until two ladies having a conversation in the intersection of a cross-aisle separated us. Adam disappeared towards the front of the store while the ladies leisurely finished their conversation. I quickly got the sense that nothing really mattered in Memphis, which was such a refreshing way of life, and a complete departure from the hectic pace of living in southern California, where "hurry" was the pejorative word.

Following what seemed like an eternity, I found Adam talking to a couple of medical students near the checkout line. They were hosting a party that afternoon and invited us to join them. Watching him, I realized how popular Adam was. He could do whatever he wanted in life and be successful. His charisma, good looks and intelligence were gifts that many young men our age were not blessed with. For a brief moment, while standing near him in the Piggly Wiggly, I felt like the luckiest guy in the world.

❧   ❧   ❧

As the Boeing jet made its way towards California, I reminisced about my introduction to Memphis. I was fascinated by the slower pace, which forced people to be polite and acknowledge one another. This way of life encouraged people to be respectful of each other, and any sense of urgency was absent … unlike the airline industry, where if a crewmember was one minute late checking in for a trip, they would be disciplined.

My sojourn to the South also provided me with a glimpse into my new friend's life. Getting to know more about Adam helped me appreciate how important it was to follow my own dreams, and how fortunate I was to have parents that encouraged me to be unafraid to follow a path that might not be popular, but would take me on a journey that would allow me to live life to its fullest … and savor every moment.

Adam's big bash to celebrate his final year of medical school was less than three weeks away. As I closed my eyes, I could still see his smiling face as he waved goodbye from the jet way door.

CHAPTER 9

As the Labor Day holiday approached, it signified the traditional end of summer. While growing up, I enjoyed spending every summer at the beach; however, fall had become my favorite time of the year. The energy created by footballs in the air as I returned to school, coupled with the brilliant colors of the changing of leaves and the aroma of mesquite wood burning in fireplaces at night helped make autumn truly something to behold. Southern California produced a magnificent second season every year that I looked forward to. Even surfing became a different experience in the fall. Waves broke further from the shore, making it more of a challenge to paddle back to ride the next wave.

Two thousand miles away, Adam and his roommate, Stephen, were decorating their townhouse in preparation for the party to celebrate Adam's final year of medical school. It had been nearly three weeks since I last saw his handsome, smiling face, and my excitement escalated as I packed for my trip to Memphis. I imagined the taste of his mouth, the scent of his body, and most of all, his incredibly charming smile.

Despite my travel schedule, Adam and I managed to visit every day by telephone. While I finished packing, my telephone bill arrived. As I opened it and glanced through the multi-page statement, I realized how exorbitant the long distance portion of my bill was … equivalent to the cost of three offline airline passes to Memphis, making me appreciate how much I missed spending time with Adam in person.

As he prepared to begin the next semester, I assumed Adam would need to repeat some of his courses because of his extended absence earlier in the year when he overdosed from taking too many sleeping pills. But when I arrived in

Memphis the afternoon of the big return to school party, I discovered things were far more serious. What I didn't realize was that Adam had been a candidate for an accredited medical school program and was being held back for another school term to achieve in three years what traditional medical school students accomplished in four years.

Because of the high grade point average Adam maintained throughout his four years of college at Middle Tennessee State University, he matriculated into the exclusive three-year medical school program which was fully subsidized by his ROTC scholarship. To help showcase Adam's success, a thumbnail sketch in a full-page ad, featuring a dashing photo of Adam in uniform, smiling and looking like the all-American college kid, appeared in newspapers throughout Arkansas, Kentucky, Missouri and Tennessee. These advertisements turned him into the role model for high school kids throughout Tennessee and surrounding southern states. Without knowing it, Adam became the poster boy for the ROTC as well as an unofficial ambassador for the College of Medicine's three-year program, when all he really wanted was to become a flight attendant and travel around the world.

The elite advanced degree program at the University of Tennessee, which accepted only fifty students a year, required doctor candidates to become accredited in six semesters (instead of the traditional eight), a feat few medical school students could even imagine accomplishing. Despite his poster boy image, academic acumen and the strong unrelenting will of his father, Adam became one of the students who did not achieve the early accreditation, something that truly devastated him. The back-to-school party he was hosting became as much of an opportunity for him to celebrate his final year of medical school as it was a chance to socialize with other medical students who were in the same program, only beginning their third—and final—year.

Although Adam was well known by most everyone at the College of Medicine, he told me that it was very difficult to return as a fourth year medical student in a three-year program. While driving from the airport to his townhouse, he explained how he felt somewhat like a failure, especially since many of his peers had already graduated and moved on to pursue their residency at hospitals all across the country.

"Unless anyone has been through what you're going through, Adam, they couldn't begin to understand the pressure you're facing," I said as I attempted to console him.

He smiled at me. "I'm so glad you are here, Will. You really know how to cheer me up."

"This can't be easy for you," I said.

"It isn't."

I flashed a smile back at him. "Will it help if I start referring to you as Dr. Adam?"

Adam nodded his head. "At this point, Will, anything will help."

Despite all of his efforts to finish medical school in record time, no one realized how unsuccessful the three-year program had become in the eyes of the medical school administration. Even Adam wasn't aware he had become a statistic that affirmed how difficult it was to complete the arduous course work in an abbreviated time frame. Ironically, the College of Medicine discontinued the accelerated program later that year, perhaps underscoring their efforts to generate superstar doctors had truly been unsuccessful.

As we arrived at Adam's townhouse, Stephen had taken command of the final preparations for the party. Several of Adam's friends had arrived early, and Stephen assigned each person to a specific task. In between the constant ringing of the telephone with people calling to confirm the time and location of the party, Adam maintained a sense of composure amongst all of the chaos.

"Come on, Will. Let's get you settled," he said, grabbing my overnight bag in one hand and leading me upstairs to his bedroom with the other. Even though the party was getting started downstairs, Adam took the time to spend a few minutes alone with me.

As we lay on his bed, he explained how he had not yet told his parents that he was going to need to continue to attend medical school for another term.

"They think I'm finishing up a couple of lab courses before beginning my residency," he said as I rubbed his shoulders, gently kissing his soft skin.

"I have to explain to them I didn't just miss a couple of classes. I failed an entire semester, which I have to make up."

"They will understand, Adam. This wasn't your fault."

"You don't know my father," he said, shaking his head. "He will not understand. There is, in his mind, no excuse for my not graduating with honors."

A knock on his door interrupted us and a tall woman with long, dark hair wearing tall black boots, a flowered blouse and dark mini-skirt opened the door. "There you are! There are a few people downstairs looking for you. I just wanted to make sure you were alright."

"Hey, Linda," Adam replied, leaning up on one arm. "We were just talking. Will, this is my friend Linda. Linda, this is Will, my friend from California."

"You're the flight attendant?" she asked.

I nodded my head, somewhat annoyed by her intrusion. Apparently Adam's friends had an open door policy.

Adam ran his hand through his long hair while Linda and I stared at one another. Seconds later, Stephen appeared alongside Linda.

"Adam, I need you at the front door. Everyone is starting to arrive."

"Okay," Adam replied. "Come on Will. It's party time."

I followed Linda and Adam down the stairs towards the living room. As Adam headed towards the front door, Linda grabbed my hand and led me through the kitchen into the family room where a large group of people had gathered. "You need to meet everyone," she said, and one by one, Linda introduced me to medical students from all across the country who were spending part of their life in Memphis. I was amazed at how many people Adam knew.

"How do you know everyone?" I asked Linda after being introduced to over two dozen students.

Her huge smile revealed a perfect set of teeth. "I'm a student advisor at the College of Medicine."

"You're the one who saved Adam's life?"

Nodding her head, I realized how much she adored Adam. "Let's get you something to drink," she said as she led me into the kitchen.

"Will, I'd like you to meet a friend of Adam's who will be moving to California at the end of the term," said Linda as she introduced me to Rich, a tall, well built physical therapist.

"Hello," I said as Rich looked me up and down.

"So you're the trolley dolly," he said as he took a swig of beer.

"Excuse me?" I said.

"He flies for Continental," said Linda.

"What's their slogan?" asked Rich. "They really move their tail for you?"

I blushed in embarrassment as Rich studied me. "Well, Linda, this one's older than most of the kids Adam brings home."

"Now Rich, be nice to Will," said Linda as she handed me a plastic cup filled with what appeared to be punch. "He doesn't get out much," Linda said, winking at me. As I took a sip from the cup, I realized it was filled with alcohol.

"I'm moving to San Diego in January," said Rich. "I'm curious if you'll move your tail for me?"

"Why? Is it in your way?"

"Ah. So you *do* have a brain. Everyone I've ever met from California seems dumber than a post. Where did you go to college?"

I couldn't believe I was being interrogated by this guy. "College? What's that? All we do in California is hang out at the beach and spend our nights at disco clubs."

Rich folded his arms and stared at me. "Are you trying to mess with me?"

"No, I'm not *trying* to. I *am* messing with you."

While the party was in full swing, packed with people, Adam saw me from across the room and waved, pointing towards the stairs. I worked my way there and met him on the landing.

"Early tomorrow, let's drive to Nashville," he said, planting a kiss on my lips. "I want to take you to Opryland."

"What's Opryland?" I asked.

"It's everything we need to take our minds off of this craziness."

❧   ❧   ❧

I wondered if Adam might introduce me to his family during our sojourn to Nashville. But instead, he introduced me to more southern-styled cooking, including grits, barbequed ribs and collard greens. Our field trip became a culinary experience that helped me appreciate how different this part of the country was.

Half way from Memphis to Nashville, we stopped at a diner along the Interstate. The hostess pointed towards a booth, and while we were looking at the menu, a girl from a nearby booth noticed us.

"Adam?" she asked.

Adam looked up and smiled. "Hey, Cherrise. What are you doing here?"

"We're heading down to Memphis. How 'bout you?"

"We're on our way to Opryland. Will is from California and has never been."

As Adam introduced us, I learned that Cherrise was his cheerleading partner in college. What a small world, I thought. But as the weekend continued to unfold, I realized that Tennessee was a very small state, and Adam had crossed paths with a lot of people. Everywhere we went, Adam bumped into people he knew … neighbors from Dickson, friends of his family, college friends as well as students from the College of Medicine, even folks that were members of his family's church congregation.

❧   ❧   ❧

As we turned onto a side road leading to the entrance of Opryland, Adam drove past the remains of a squirrel that appeared to have been run over. A flower had been placed near the body of the squirrel. I was struck by the way in which people from the South regarded how precious life was. Unlike California, people in Tennessee took the time to recognize every living creature. Where I lived, people just drove over something without any regard to whether or not the being had a purpose. Spending time with Adam helped me better understand the quality of life.

The highlight of our trip was visiting the world famous Grand Old Opry, where for generations, country music legends have stood on stage and performed their magic. This evening, Minnie Pearl, Crystal Gayle and Dolly Parton were all scheduled to perform, and Adam had arranged for us to watch the show from the wings of the stage, which gave me a much different perspective of the storied auditorium. As each of the performers arrived near the stage, they spoke to us and asked how we were doing. Adam introduced me to each of them and explained I was visiting from California. Minnie Pearl gave me a huge hug to welcome me. Crystal Gayle admired me with a very seductive look and then flashed a smile that could melt a pound of butter. But it was Dolly Parton who stole my heart. "Will, I'm so glad you came to visit us," she said as she hugged me. I could barely breathe as I contained my excitement. "Adam, you're so adorable. I hope you boys have a lot of fun tonight."

Fun was something Adam taught me a lot about. Spending time at Opryland gave us a chance to be kids again. After spending the afternoon at the theme park, we walked through the children's park, admiring the varied collection of animals and livestock. We eventually ended up walking along the Mississippi River as a full moon surrounded us.

"What's it like to fly anywhere you want to go?" Adam asked.

"It's nice ... especially when you have someone to travel with."

"Wouldn't it be great if we could fly to a place far away up in the sky where we could float on a cloud all alone?"

I nodded my head as my heart skipped a beat. Spending a moment alone with him was all I wanted to do. I glanced up and noticed the Little Dipper.

Adam followed my eyes as I looked up at the stars, and he put his arm around me. "Will, no matter where I am, we will never be far apart. All you have to do is glance up towards the sky, look at the stars and then you can feel me close to you. Because the same stars I can see will be the ones you are look-ing at."

The following afternoon, I left with memories of the weekend in Nashville clearly etched in my mind. Returning to California, I often reminisced upon my visit with Adam as I endured a very difficult couple of months. Following nearly a year and a half of contract negotiations, Continental pilots began a thirty-day cooling off period. On October twenty-third, the Air Line Pilots Association elected to strike Continental, and the airline immediately ceased all flight operations. It was the first work stoppage in the company's forty-two year history.

Twenty days later, with Thanksgiving and Christmas fast approaching, the pilots and Continental reached an agreement on a new labor contract. While flight operations resumed on November the sixteenth, service was gradually restored, and because I had less than six months seniority, I remained indefi-nitely furloughed. Unfortunately, until I returned to work, I could not use any of my pass benefits; therefore, I remained grounded in southern California to enjoy the holidays with my family.

Traditional Thanksgiving for me consisted of a mid-afternoon dinner at my parents' home, followed by a walk along the beach at sunset. Both of my par-ents were raised in the Midwest, so the enjoyment of a long walk on the beach during late November, when the rest of the country was suffering from inclem-ent weather, was their way of appreciating something they never could while living in Chicago.

Returning home around nine o'clock on Thanksgiving eve, a telegram from Continental was waiting for me, recalling me to work effective New Year's Day. Elated with this good news, I was even more jubilant to receive a late night tele-phone call from Adam.

"How was your Thanksgiving?" he asked.

"It was good," I said. "After dinner, we all went for a walk along the beach. It kind of felt like you were here."

Adam sighed. "I wish I was there, Will. And soon, we'll be together again. But I've got to finish some lab work before Monday …" His voice trailed off, and the distance between California and Memphis seemed much further than two thousand miles.

"What are your plans for Christmas?" I asked.

"I haven't even thought about it. My parents are expecting me in Dickson, but I've got a lot of studying I need to do."

I was silent as Adam's shallow breathing echoed against the telephone line.

"Will, now is not a good time for me."

Sensing his exhaustion, I tempered my enthusiasm about returning to work at the end of the year. "I'm probably going to head up to my parent's cottage at Lake Tahoe on Monday. There isn't a phone up there, but I can call you from the pay phone at the market Monday night."

"When are you going back to work?"

"Not 'til January."

"Maybe we can do something during winter break at the end of January?"

"I'll bid for the end of the month off."

"Okay, Will. I've got to get some sleep. I really miss you."

"I miss you, too," I replied.

❈   ❈   ❈

While driving up to Lake Tahoe, the weather forecast promised another cold week. The lake was frozen over and the trees were white with snow as I arrived at my family's cottage. A sense of joy filled the air as I glanced up at the large Douglas fir tree next to the cottage. Through the setting sun, a star's shadow illuminated the lake. I remembered what Adam had promised me about the stars, and surrounded by the snow, I felt the warmth of his love. Through the haze of dusk, I envisioned Adam looking up towards the sky to see the same stars I saw.

The following week, Continental announced the January flight attendant schedules. I was thrilled when I was awarded a schedule with only three four-day trips and a turnaround trip to Denver on New Year's Day, giving me the last eleven days of the month off to spend with Adam during winter break. And to add to my excitement, I learned that I would be flying again with my friend Helen. Nineteen seventy-seven was going to be a good year.

CHAPTER 10

What should have been a simple turnaround trip turned into a mini-nightmare. The two-hour flight from Los Angeles on New Year's Day left on time, but was over an hour late arriving in Denver due to a snow storm which blanketed the Rockies. The packed wide-body aircraft was tossed about like a football, and mid-way through the meal service, the Captain ordered the cabin crew to take their seats. Many of the passengers became ill, and between meal trays and overflowing air sickness bags scattered throughout the cabin, our arrival in Denver was a welcome relief.

To make matters worse, Continental's extensive route structure was greatly impacted by the severe weather problems, and the storm wreaked havoc on holiday travelers throughout the Continental system.

My return trip to California departed over two hours late, and the passengers were not happy as they boarded the McDonnell Douglas jet. As I was assigned to work in the first class galley, I sequestered myself behind the galley curtain and avoided any passenger contact.

I returned home after dark on New Year's Day and slept for most of the next day before getting up to return to the airport for the first of three four-day trips I was scheduled to work during the month. Flying alongside of Helen made the trip bearable, and she consoled me as I confided how much I missed Adam, sharing my frustration at not being able to spend any part of the holidays with him.

Following my trip, which included layovers in Chicago, Las Vegas and Miami, I left behind the warm tropical breezes of the southeast as a winter rain storm surrounded Los Angeles, bringing with it cool temperatures. Returning home just after noon, I left my suitcase in the hallway and took a quick shower before finally snuggling into my own bed. Wishing I was on a lay-over in Honolulu, I imagined walking with Adam along Waikiki Beach near Diamond Head. Shortly after my wish became a dream, the warm tropical breeze surrounding me in my dream was interrupted by the distant ringing of my telephone. On the fifth ring, I clumsily reached for the phone.

"Is this Will?" asked a man with a southern accent.

"Uh huh," I said, sleepily.

"It's Stephen Green, Adam's roommate, calling from Memphis."

"Hi," I managed to say, attempting to sound coherent.

"I am so very sorry to call with such terrible news."

I was silent as Stephen breathed heavily into the phone.

"Adam took his own life this afternoon."

The words stung my brain, which was attempting to comprehend what Stephen had just said. "What?" I asked in disbelief.

"He was found in his car earlier today."

As the reality of what Stephen was telling me began to sink in, I sat up in bed. "Stephen, what happened?"

"Oh, Will ... I'm afraid I don't know. The police haven't given us any information. All I know is they found Adam in his car out in Shelby Forest. They're going to do an autopsy to determine—"

"—So he's really gone?"

Stephen was silent as my question echoed off of the telephone line. "Yes, Will. He's dead."

My immediate thought was to call someone ... anyone ... who could help make Adam better. Surely there was a doctor somewhere who could fix whatever was wrong.

"I'm so sorry," said Stephen as I stared at the beige wall of my bedroom. "His family is planning a service, but I think it will be up in Dickson."

Tears began to stream down my face. I didn't even hear what Stephen was saying.

"Shall I call you once I have more information?"

"Yes, Stephen. Please do. Where is Adam right now?" I asked.

"He's downtown ... in the morgue."

❦   ❦   ❦

I could hardly breathe. Adam had taken his own life, and all I wanted to do was hold him tightly and tell him how much I loved him.

My friend Timmy was who I called first to share the incomprehensible news.

"Are they sure it was a suicide?" he asked when I relayed what little I knew.

After I admitted it was more than likely Adam had taken his own life, Timmy attempted to put things in perspective.

"Will, just be glad you didn't quit your job and move to Tennessee," he said. "Then you'd be stuck in Memphis without a job … and a boyfriend."

"Adam is gone," I said as tears rolled down my face. "And I don't think I can even make it to his funeral."

"Why not?"

In my state of confusion, I tried to explain to Timmy that my life wasn't that simple. Even if I decided to go to Adam's funeral, it would have been difficult to get the time off from work. Continental had guidelines concerning requesting personal time off to attend a funeral, and same sex relationships were not included in the personnel policies at that time. In fact, the only real option I had was to call in sick, which was something I never considered doing because I would have needed to request an emergency pass to get to Tennessee on another airline since Continental didn't fly there. Traveling on a pass while on sick leave would have put me at risk for disciplinary action, so a geographic obstacle was present by design. I found myself between a rock and a hard place.

During the next three days, while I sought refuge by memorializing him on my own, Adam's family realized just how well liked he was as an outpouring of sympathy was expressed by an assortment of friends and colleagues from the University of Tennessee College of Medicine.

Adam's mother displayed incredible strength as she prepared for the funeral. However, Adam's father did not participate in making any of the funeral and burial arrangements, which placed an inordinate amount of stress on Adam's mother. Perhaps one of the most difficult parts of planning for Adam's funeral was searching for something suitable for him to wear. While shopping in Dickson's one and only men's clothing store for a burial suit, the sales clerk was exuberant and poured over Adam's mother and sister while they browsed for an appropriate outfit. After pressing them for details about who they were shopping for, Adam's sister Carol explained they were shopping for her brother. The sales clerk wanted to know where he lived and what his tastes were. Finally, Adam's sister blurted out the harsh reality. "He's dead," she said as Adam's mother remained stoic while the sales clerk flushed with embarrassment.

Stephen, Adam's roommate, called me once the funeral had been scheduled for Saturday afternoon. Helen, my flying partner, encouraged me to fly to Nashville and attend the funeral. "Will, you need to let his family know how much he meant to you. And I think it will bring you some closure if you go."

But I was resistant. I couldn't find the courage to fly to Tennessee because I was having difficulty grasping the fact that Adam was really gone. The closest I had come to facing the death of someone my own age was losing a classmate in high school who was killed in an automobile accident. However, Adam's death was not an accident, which made it even more difficult for me to accept. But what I was really avoiding was facing the hard core reality of his death. I didn't want to view Adam's reposed body in a coffin. I couldn't bear the thought of seeing his casket being lowered into a hole in the ground. It was simply easier for me to deny he was gone altogether.

Despite my not wanting to accept the obvious, a part of me wanted to just wash Adam out of my mind. I was angry that he did not share with me his decision to end his life. How could he have been in so much despair and not bothered to let me know? The fact that he never called to say goodbye became a dilemma in my mind and filled my head with angst. While my heart was aching, my brain was racing. I wanted more than anything to understand why Adam felt there was no alternative except to take his own life.

There was also my fear that I would be extremely out of place at the funeral. Where would I sit? The funeral home chapel had an area set off to the side for family members, but I had not even met Adam's parents. Since Adam had never shared our relationship with his family, coupled with the fact that his father was reclusive in the first place, my decision about whether or not to attend Adam's funeral bounced back and forth like a tennis ball in a political debate.

Avoiding the emotional pain was something done effortlessly in the seventies. While many of my friends encouraged me to just smoke a joint to mellow out, I retreated to the two things which brought me comfort … music and surfing. The lyrics of some of the most heart-wrenching ballads ever written provided me solitude while riding waves along Sunset Beach in Orange County. I found a sense of resolve that took me back to the place where I taught Adam how to surf. Ironically, paddling in the Pacific Ocean, waiting for the right wave to ride to shore, provided me with a sense of sanctity. This was one place where nothing had a hold on me, a place where I was invincible.

When I stopped off at my parents' house before heading home Friday afternoon, my mother sensed something was wrong, yet I could not bring myself to tell her that Adam had taken his own life. It was something people in Orange County would not understand. Even when asked if everything was okay, I denied my pain and simply excused my lackluster demeanor as having had a rough trip earlier in the week.

"Did you hear the news?" my mother asked. "The White House expects President Carter to pardon the Vietnam War draft evaders."

"What about all of the conscientious objectors?" I asked. "They should be pardoned as well."

"That's a very good point, dear, which will undoubtedly stir yet another protest. Why don't you stay for dinner? Your father is out of town and I'm having the Moore's over. Their daughter, Sharon, flies for American and they're trying to persuade me to go with them on a Windjammer cruise."

"Thanks, Mom … I just don't think I would be good company."

My mother had recently celebrated her fiftieth birthday and was contemplating going on a barefoot cruise. She had the energy of someone much younger, and her positive attitude and enthusiasm helped to lift my depressed spirit.

Because neither of my parents knew how much I cared for Adam, they could not appreciate how desperate I was to publicly mourn the loss of the man I had fallen in love with. Since I didn't turn to my mother or my father for the emotional support I needed, I found refuge in knowing I would return to work, where transported across the country on a seven-twenty-seven jet filled with strangers in their own world—facing problems which were far greater than my own—the loss of Adam would somehow diminish at thirty-one thousand feet.

However, by not attending Adam's funeral, I deprived myself of witnessing a tremendous outpouring of love and affection for someone who had stolen my heart. In retrospect, I would have been overwhelmed by the amount of people attending his funeral, and just as his family discovered … how much Adam was admired, loved and respected. Doctors, medical students, friends and even a few patients Adam had treated all convened in Dickson from throughout Tennessee, Mississippi and Arkansas. Instead of witnessing an unforgettable memorial, I mourned in private two thousand miles away, unable to share my grief with those who adored the man I loved.

At his funeral, one of Adam's medical professors talked about loss, and while he alluded to the fact that Adam's death could have been prevented, he spoke about how one can usually sense the pain when someone is unhappy with life. What was different is Adam deceived us into believing he was not in any kind of pain, preventing all of us from becoming cognizant of his despair.

On Saturday, while Adam's funeral was underway, the postal service delivered my mail, which included a white envelope with a Memphis postmark. As I glanced at the familiar handwriting, I was jarred. The envelope was postmarked the day Adam took his life.

Trembling, I opened the envelope to find a neatly written letter, dated the day before Adam drove to Shelby Forest.

ᖆ

Dear Will,

I hope you are doing well. I really miss you!

I look forward to walking on the beaches of Hawaii with you soon.

I'm thinking of you, always ...

Love,

Adam

❦   ❦   ❦

I needed to get out of my apartment, so I called Timmy.

"Will, come up and spend the night here. We'll go to brunch tomorrow at the Farmers' Market and then head to the beach. And see how you feel tomorrow afternoon. You're more than welcome to stay here if you want to call in sick for your trip."

Arriving at Timmy's apartment, I was still trying to understand the letter from Adam. Timmy, on the other hand, could hardly contain his excitement. "Remember me telling you about Mark, the cute guy I met at Studio One last weekend?"

"Yeah," I said, even though I couldn't remember any of Timmy's liaison's names, since he grew tired of them after one date and was on to the next one before I could remember the last one's name.

"He's the guy who works at the Universal Amphitheater."

I nodded my head. "He works backstage?"

"No. The box office."

"He's going to UCLA?"

"Business School at USC."

"Of course. I remember."

"He got us a pair of tickets to see Olivia Newton-John."

"When is she performing?"

"Tonight," said Timmy, jumping up and down with excitement. "Eight o'clock. Fourth row center."

The thought of going to a concert made me feel less anxious, especially because Timmy's taste in music was less than eclectic, which was just what I needed.

"We can have dinner at Casita Del Campo in Silver Lake. I can feel a margarita moonlight starting to shine."

Despite making bad choices with his bed fellows, Timmy was a wonderful friend, and he did his best to keep my mind focused on things other than missing Adam's funeral.

After two rounds of margaritas at the bar, we were seated adjacent to a group of a dozen guys celebrating a birthday. Timmy flirted with Greg, the birthday boy, and before I had a chance to even glance at the menu, a pitcher of margaritas was sent our way. By the time we ordered dinner, we had become part of the birthday celebration. Greg, we quickly learned, had just been hired as a Continental flight attendant.

"What a coincidence," screamed Timmy. "Will works for the Proud Bird, too."

On cue, the dozen guys began to sing the tune from Continental's infamous ad campaign.

> *We're here to make you happy*
> *We're out to make you pleased*
> *You're flying Continental*
> *Your flight will be a breeze*
> *We'll help to make you happy*
> *We'll skip to prove it's true*
> *On Continental Airlines*
> *We move our tails for you ...*
> *We really move our tails for you*
> *We make your every wish come true*

Fly Continental Airlines
We really move our tails for you

Other diners surrounding us applauded our brief vocal performance. Greg flashed a smile towards me. "Where are you based?"

"Here," I replied, sipping my margarita.

"We need to get to know one another," Greg said as he raised his glass and winked at me. "Here's to new friends and new places."

I raised my glass and attempted to smile. While toasting Greg, I wondered if Adam was in a better place and silently wished I could somehow receive a clue or a message that he was okay.

Had it not been for the fact that Timmy's friend Mark was expecting us at the Amphitheater, we would have followed the birthday party home from the restaurant. Driving to Universal City, Timmy couldn't stop talking about Greg. I was in awe at how easily Timmy could move from one man to the next without missing a beat.

Meanwhile, I was deep in thought about the letter Adam had written. Did he intend to come to California and then fly to Hawaii with me or was the letter his way of saying good-bye? How I wished for some clarity so I could understand what Adam was thinking. Instead of getting answers, I surrounded myself with music.

Watching Olivia Newton-John perform was magical. Because we were seated only twenty feet from the stage, I felt as if she was singing to me. Performing from her repertoire of hit songs which spanned an eleven-year career, Olivia closed her two-act concert by singing her signature song *I Honestly Love You*. The lyric resonated deep inside my mind all the way back to West Hollywood.

❦   ❦   ❦

Despite Timmy's suggestion that I take some time off, I elected to fly my scheduled trip the following night. Helen encouraged me to talk about how I felt as we flew to Houston, but all I could do was keep the pain buried deep inside of my soul. I was angry at Adam for leaving us, and furious with his friends for not doing something to prevent him from taking his own life.

While continuing our trip from Houston to Miami, I was confronted by a passenger who complained about being served a snack box instead of a hot meal (like the man in front of him). Continental had just introduced a new advertising campaign that accompanied extremely lower fares in highly competitive markets. Dubbed "Chickenfeed Fares," passengers that traditionally could only afford to travel via bus were finding their way on to Continental airplanes. As tactfully as possible, I explained to the unhappy man that coach passengers paid a much higher fare, and therefore were provided a hot meal. I offered him a complimentary cocktail, which he declined. While he sulked for the remainder of the flight, I became more compassionate towards passengers because I realized how little I knew about what they might be going through emotionally. Even though I was dying inside, I managed to put on my uniform and serve meals and drinks with a smile, creating the impression that the world was perfect … when, in fact, it was crumbling all around me.

While on the lay-over in Miami, I joined Helen at a screening of the recently-released movie *A Star Is Born*, which focused on the tremendous waste of a life. Helen reminded me it was just a Hollywood movie, and a remake at that. I explained that because art imitates reality, it comforted me to know I wasn't alone in experiencing loss. It helped me endure the pain of Adam's death. However, instead of expressing my anger, I felt vulnerable and was afraid to let anyone near my heart. In some ways, I was much like Adam in that I did not have a support system to provide a safety net if I fell.

A few weeks later, I went to Little Poppy Beach to watch the sunset. As I sat on the rocks, watching the sailboats return to Newport Harbor, I reflected upon the time Adam and I sat in this very same spot, and how he was in awe of the natural beauty of this very special place. As I thought about him, a butterfly lit on my shoulder and comforted me, almost as if she was delivering a message that everything would be okay.

While the sun disappeared behind the Palos Verdes peninsula, I returned home and wrote a lyric which expressed just how much I missed Adam. I asked the never-answered question: why did he leave us?

Ode to Adam

I was sitting here, all alone
In this spot where we sat not too long ago
And a butterfly stopped, and lit on me
Almost as if she knew I was thinking of you.

She must have seen the expression on my face
Or the sad look in my eyes.
"Where is our friend? Why did he go away?"
I don't know ... Happy and at peace, I hope
No one knows why ... We never will.

It's been a month, four weeks, twenty days
I still weep ... I'm still sad, but I think I realize
You did what you wanted to do for you.

The butterfly left, as did you, without saying goodbye
Will I ever know why you didn't love life?
For you had so much Adam ...
So much ... maybe too much?
Thank you for sharing a little with me.

CHAPTER 11

The gentle beeping that emanated from the alarm clock in my suite at the Opryland Hotel brought me back to present day. As hotel alarm clocks go, this was one of the better ones. It wasn't ear piercing or earth shattering. It was almost soothing ... yet it did the job. I was awake.

I stared at the warm yellow walls of the bedroom as I comprehended the enormity of my dream. Had I really just spent eight hours reliving highlights of six months of my life? Sitting up, I glanced towards the window. It was bright outside, but I couldn't tell if it was sunshine or just the illusion of light peeking into my room from the hotel's constantly lit faux courtyard. Rubbing my head, I wondered if I could still be dreaming.

Had I created the opportunity to travel back in time? The reality of my dream made me ponder the possibility. Was I capable of transporting myself back to an earlier time in my life simply by being in the same place at a different time?

My stomach growled, helping me realize I was definitely awake and not dreaming. I slowly maneuvered my tired body out of bed and unpacked clothes for my presentation at the tourism conference. Realizing my hunger pain stemmed from not having eaten since yesterday's flight from Los Angeles, I contemplated ordering breakfast from room service. Then I remembered I was staying at a three-thousand room convention hotel and it took me nearly twenty minutes to find my suite with detailed directions when I arrived yesterday. Plan B was the better way to go, and I reached for a long-sleeved T-shirt and pair of jeans while I reflected upon my dream. The image of Adam appeared once again like a movie in my mind.

It took me only five minutes to find a coffee shop in the same wing of the hotel as my suite. Julie, my server, brought me coffee while I studied the menu. Given my state of hunger, I decided to order a cheese omelet with vegetables, grits and a side of Hickory-smoked bacon. One of the luxuries of doing a book tour was being able to order things to eat that were too messy to make at home. As much as I loved bacon, every time I prepared it, my house smelled like a fast food restaurant several days later. Julie nodded her head approvingly when I ordered the side of bacon.

The headline of *The Tennessean* featured an update on the death toll from the war in Iraq. While scanning the front page story, I was reminded that war is such an evil thing, and of how similar this conflict was to the Vietnam war thirty years ago. Like most Americans, I was awestruck by the incomprehensible cost of defending our freedom, yet I was frustrated at my inability to do anything to improve the situation. And, like most everyone else, I just turned the page and continued to glance at other news stories, wishing the war would simply disappear altogether.

On page four, an entertainment business story caught my attention. Paramount Pictures' new president was implementing a strategic marketing plan to help jump start the studio's lackluster year. I read the story with great interest because for over a decade I had worked for Paramount and had a vested interest in the studio's success: my retirement plan. According to the newspaper story, Mr. Black, the new studio president, was adamant about his goal to turn the studio's balance sheet around to be the same color as his name. Viacom, Paramount's parent company, had become a major force in the entertainment industry and demanded a significant return on their investment, no matter what it took. Mr. Black's position was clear. He was changing the way in which the studio developed new projects, which was to refrain from taking risks or thinking outside of the traditional boundaries. Effective immediately, television shows, movies and theme park development was to be done based on previously established formula-driven success models. Mr. Black was quoted about these efforts, stating the studio was now planning to emulate the success of cookie cutter entertainment homogenization, similar to what was implemented during the nineteen eighties by the Walt Disney Company. From reading the story, it appeared that instead of competing to be an innovative leader in the entertainment industry, Paramount—the oldest working motion picture studio in Hollywood—was about to step back and embark on a path that would paint the studio as moribund and lacking the creative luster that was a prerequisite to success.

Julie delivered my breakfast as I finished reading the Paramount story. In between savoring each bite of my omelet, my mind flashed back to nineteen eighty-one, when I made the decision to depart the airline industry and join a debut television news program designed to present entertainment industry news six nights a week. Based on Paramount's Hollywood lot, the concept of the new show featured a magazine format, with stories presented by Ron Hendren and Dixie Whatley, supported by half a dozen news bureaus across the country, including one in London. Celebrity gossip columnist Rona Barrett also made regular appearances on the broadcast, named Entertainment Tonight. The thirty-minute broadcast was presented in four acts, including an eight to ten-minute segment dubbed the "Inside Cover Story," featuring a story of interest which was traditionally breaking entertainment news.

I was hired to manage the news bureau in San Francisco, providing production support for developing stories throughout the Pacific Northwest. San Francisco was an emerging entertainment media capital with an impressive slate of movies being filmed in and around the city as well as a variety of post-production work. The music scene was another significant source of activity, and my bureau produced at least one ten-minute segment every week for the new show. San Francisco and the music scene in the early eighties was a metamorphosis since the city was the birthplace of rock and roll. Our formula for each segment was quite simple. We took risks and created stories that were cutting edge. Following our first season, the show was nominated for several Emmy awards, including the most newsworthy investigative news segment. Reminiscing about this part of my career made me proud of my accomplishments and the legacy I left for those who followed in my footsteps, even if segment producers would now be required to develop cookie-cutter stories.

The transition from flying for Continental to working on a television show was an easy one as many of the people I dealt with were as challenging as the flying public had become. I had no difficulty working with unique personalities, and because Entertainment Tonight quickly became a well-known news program by the end of its first season, working on the show had a certain cache.

Being affiliated with a major motion picture studio also provided some cool perks, including working the red carpet at award shows, attending movie premieres and going to concerts that my friends couldn't get tickets to. However, like working for Continental, my schedule varied from segment to segment, the hours were long, and I traveled wherever the story took me. While San Francisco was home, I lived out of a suitcase.

"More coffee?" asked Julie as I finished my breakfast.

"Thanks," I replied as she refilled my coffee mug.

"Are you here for the conference?" she asked.

I nodded my head as Julie cleared my plate.

"So many people are here from all over the country," she said. "Where are you from?"

A familiar-sounding voice interrupted us. "Will, is that you?"

I turned to discover the woman I sat next to on the flight to Nashville yesterday. "Hello, Karen," I said as I stood to shake her hand.

"I would like you to meet my friend Carol Smith," Karen said in her upbeat way. "Carol is the bride's mother."

I extended my hand to hers.

"Karen told me you're a published writer," said Carol, shaking my hand. "It's a real pleasure to meet you."

"Thank you," I replied. "I understand the wedding is happening later today?"

"Yes. At four o'clock ... in the rotunda on the river walk, near the Old Hickory Plantation House."

I nodded my head as I remembered discovering the picturesque spot during my book signing reception last night.

"We just came from the spa," said Karen. "You must try the hot stone massage treatment, Will. It's a life-altering experience."

I smiled and nodded my head.

"And the massage therapist taught me how to breathe," Karen said quite matter-of-factly, before providing me with a brief overview about how most of us breathe through our chest, while some people breathe through their stomach, and anyone who is emotionally connected breathes through their gut. "How do you breathe, Will?" she asked me.

Taken aback by her question, I stared in disbelief. "I'm not sure, Karen. I guess I'm one of those people that breathe through their nose."

Carol smiled as I attempted to digest my omelet as well as this new information about breathing and massage therapy. "Karen mentioned you are from California?"

"Yes, I live in Santa Monica ... in southern California. How about you? Are you from Nashville?"

"No. Actually, I'm from Dickson. It's a small town nearby."

"I know where Dickson is. I knew someone who was going to medical school in Memphis back in the seventies. He was from Dickson."

"It's such a small world," said Karen. "Carol's brother went to medical school in Memphis."

"Where does your friend practice?" Carol asked, curiously.

"Unfortunately, he died while he was in medical school," I said. "In nineteen seventy-seven."

Carol blinked in silence and turned pale, almost as if she had seen a ghost.

Karen raised her hand to her mouth and took a deep breath, exhaling from her stomach.

"What was his name?" asked Carol.

"Adam," I said.

"You knew my brother?" she asked, shaking her head in disbelief.

Throughout my life, I have never doubted that chance meetings are more than coincidence. Our paths cross with certain people by design. Now, nearly thirty years after Adam died, I was having coffee with his sister. Being this close to him after three decades felt almost surreal. Because I wasn't able to spend time with Adam during the final weeks of his life, getting to know his sister helped me process a significant loss from my past.

While we studied one another, I explained to Carol that meeting her brother on that Bicentennial Fourth of July weekend forever changed my life.

"I was always curious about who his friends were," Carol said as she sipped her coffee. "So many people came to his funeral, but I was still in shock and don't remember much of anything, except how well-liked Adam was … and how many friends he had."

I nodded my head.

"He was so popular. Unfortunately, most of Adam's friends went on with their lives after he died, and eventually my mother lost touch with everyone he knew."

As I listened to her, I couldn't help but wonder what it must have been like for Adam's family to deal with losing him. Although he was only twenty-five years old when he died, he was an adult who could not face the social pressures imposed by his unforgiving father. While other options existed besides suicide, Adam's decision to end his life served no purpose other than to inflict heartache upon everyone who knew him. The only thing his death accomplished was to free him from his own personal pain.

Carol's freshly manicured fingers surrounded her coffee mug as she reminisced. "I remember someone wrote a poem after Adam died. Stephen, his roommate when he lived in Memphis, had the poem typeset onto parchment paper and sent it to us."

My heart skipped a beat as Carol acknowledged my literary attempt to say goodbye to Adam. I confessed I was the author of the poem. Even though we had never before met, I took comfort knowing Adam's family eventually learned there was someone from California who was very much a part of his life.

Carol leaned across the table and touched my hand. "Will, you have no idea how much that poem meant to my mother. It hung on the wall in her bedroom until the day she died."

❦   ❦   ❦

Four hours later, as the bridal party was lining up in formation near the rotunda, my publicist brushed a piece of lint from the lapel of my black Donna Karan jacket, which I wore over a crisp black button-down dress shirt. Accompanied by black slacks and black Kenneth Cole shoes, I looked like I was ready to address a group of Hollywood agents instead of three thousand travel industry professionals.

"You okay?" Jenn asked in her reassuring, maternal way.

"Yeah," I replied. "Although as much as I dislike group events, I would rather be attending the wedding of Carol's daughter right now."

"Did you even know he had a sister?"

I nodded my head as I glanced at the talking points I had written for my address to the tourism conference. "Adam talked about her frequently. He said she was the best thing his parents produced. Adam told me Carol had their mother's charm and intuitiveness as well as the perseverance and determined will of their father."

"Was it weird spending time with her?"

"Not at all, Jenn. It was actually quite nice. In a way, I feel as though Adam is back in my life."

As the president of the Travel Industry Association of America introduced me to the audience, I glanced at Jenn. "It's show time," she said.

I walked onto the stage with my blue index cards tucked safely in the breast pocket of my jacket. I was surprised to see so many people in the audience. My heart began to race as I took a deep breath and smiled.

"Good afternoon, everyone," I said as the welcoming applause began to subside. "It is such an honor to be here today in the country music capital of the world."

As a small applause responded to my acknowledgement of Nashville, I glanced offstage towards Jenn, who gave me a thumbs up.

"For those of you who have no clue who I am or why I was invited to speak to you today, join the club. I, too, was curious when I got the call to speak at this very impressive collection of travel professionals. 'Why me?' I asked. Then I discovered what this convention is all about, which is sharing experiences and telling stories. Somehow, my background makes me the perfect speaker.

"To qualify as a person that understands the travel industry, I should mention I began my working career long ago as a reservations agent before securing the much coveted job of flight attendant back in the day before deregulation forever changed the airline industry. From there, I flew as fast as I could to the entertainment industry, where I became a production coordinator for a start up news program, which years later became a leader in the entertainment industry and a household name. After a decade of producing stories for Entertainment Tonight, I became a freelance journalist and traveled all over the world covering stories that I found compelling and interesting.

"My friends will tell you they think of me as somewhat of a bon vivant, but in reality, I am simply the consummate frequent flyer. I belong to three dozen frequent traveler programs and maintain a current guest profile with every major hotel chain and rental car company. Having flown to every continent in the world, I am fortunate to stand here today and tell you how important this industry is.

"Back when I was celebrating the quarter century mark of my life, I set out to explore Hawaii. On my first trans-Pacific flight, I sat behind two elderly ladies who were also on their maiden voyage, a trip each of them had always talked about with their husbands. Something always came up, preventing them from taking that coveted journey, and now both ladies were widows, and they were crossing the Pacific without their husbands. I remember thinking how sad they didn't do what they had always dreamed of doing when the opportunity arose.

"That story reminds me of my first trip to South Africa and a safari through Botswana. I contemplated not going on the trip because I was terrified by the possibility of being mauled by a lion, trampled by an elephant, or killed by a rhinoceros. But the possibility of missing this very special corner of the world persuaded my sense of adventure to prevail, and the trip became one of the most spiritual journeys I have ever taken. One night, while I sat around a campfire enjoying the company of five other travel journalists, we looked up at the stars and I felt a sense of belonging. Many years ago, a friend of mine told me no matter where in the world I was, I could take comfort looking up at the sky and seeing the same stars that he saw. What I didn't realize was the constellation I was observing was different than what I saw from the deck of my California beach house. But the thought that stars guide us through our journey, no matter how far we travel, has served as an indelible road map for my entire life.

"I leave with you one important piece of advice … and that is to never lose sight of providing a memorable experience to everyone you cross paths with … and enjoy life to the fullest, savoring every moment."

❧   ❧   ❧

As I left the stage, I remembered Adam telling me to look up at the sky and observe the stars … the same stars he could see from Tennessee. The last time I visited Adam, he taught me to live in the moment. After three decades, one thing was abundantly clear: my affection for him had not diminished.

In many ways, it made perfect sense that I got to know Adam in the blues capital of our country. All that music surrounded us as we talked about our desire to travel all over the world. The only thing different between us was that I survived the social pressures we each faced, and through my perseverance, I discovered that life was worth living, and the world was filled with so many exciting people and places.

EPILOGUE

Before leaving Nashville, I drove to Dickson to visit Adam's gravesite. The storm that had produced a little snow earlier in the week had left the South, and headstones were visible as I entered the cemetery. Driving to the spot where Adam had been laid to rest nearly three decades before, I stopped the engine of my rental car and slowly walked towards his family's plot.

A cold breeze whipped through the cemetery and made me shiver. Standing near his headstone, I was numb. As I reflected upon the memory of someone I had once deeply loved, a certain sadness surrounded me. I was overcome once again by the waste of a precious life. Adam was someone who brought so much joy to others and lit up any room he entered. His sister said that Adam was the perfect person. "He gave us a sense of hope ... of how things could be. That life is what you make of it."

By introducing me to Memphis and the South, he forever changed my life. I remembered the first time I saw Adam at Studio One, when he asked me to dance with him as the DJ cued "The Hustle." No one would have ever believed I had the courage to get on that cavernous dance floor, but Adam made it seem effortless. He made anything possible. Remembering that moment in time, I reminisced about how much I wanted to explore the world with this handsome young man. During his visit to California, he asked me to help him realize his dream to see the world in a day. To ride a moon beam and fly to a place far away up in the sky where we would float on a cloud all alone. Adam believed that by drifting in space, we could be lost in a love of our own ... and that it might last forever.

I was one person who loved him and wanted nothing in return. Losing him fractured my heart ... and forced me to develop a timidity that kept me from getting close to anyone for a very long time. After Adam died, I feared that love was nothing more than just a prelude to sorrow. I found myself looking for someone who laughed like him, convinced that someday, somewhere I would find love again. In my heart, I wondered if I would overcome the pain. In my dreams, I always hoped I would discover a new love, and in time I did begin to trust in love again. Eventually I realized how we grow stronger through the pain and capturing that moment has been my life's work.

Several hours later, I bid farewell to Nashville and continued on my book tour. Looking out at the clouds which blanketed the farmlands far below, I wondered how my life would have changed if Adam had not taken his own life that January morning in nineteen seventy-seven. Would he have left Memphis to discover how beautiful the beaches of Hawaii were and visit those faraway places he talked about … or would he have completed medical school and become an Army doctor? My mind flashed upon the image of Adam wearing a lab jacket with his name embroidered on the front pocket. I envisioned him kneeling down to console a young girl who had broken her arm.

"What color should we paint your arm?" he asked.

"Casts don't come in colors, do they?" asked the girl, curiously.

"Well, we can make it any color you want," Adam said reassuringly. "I think you would look quite pretty in pink, don't you?"

The colors of rainbows leaving the world far behind was all I could see as the jet headed into the sunset. I closed my eyes and drifted off to sleep. In my subconscious state of mind, I could hear Adam whispering in my ear, "Will, have another dream on me."

While I will never know what might have happened, the world was forever changed by the few short years Adam was here, and remembering that brief moment in my life will always bring a smile to my face.

Why should I long for what I know
Can never be revealed to me?
I only pray that I may grow
As sure and bravely as a tree.

I do not ask why tireless grief
Remains, or why all beauty flies;
I only crave the blind relief
Of branches groping towards the skies.

Let me bring every seed to fruit,
Sharing, whatever comes to pass
The strong persistence of the root,
The patient courage of the grass.

Heartened by every source of mirth,
I shall not mind the wounds and scars,
Feeling the soul strengthen of earth,
The bright conviction of the stars.
—Louis Untermeyer

Acknowledgements

This book came to life through the love and support of Carol Crosby Smith, who trusted in me to revive the memory of her brother. Writing this book helped me realize that losing someone at such a young age is something you don't forget. The pain you experience is tumultuous, overwhelming and never ending.

Two years ago, my friend Irene Silva encouraged me to tell this story, and throughout this incredible story-telling journey, she has been a constant source of encouragement and support.

More than a mensch, Glenn Enos continues to be an anchor of support and a pillar of undeniable strength. Thank you for always being here for me, G. Each and every day, you make life worth living, and I am beyond fortunate to have you in my life.

Kudos to Patricia Nelson and Alex Padilla for keeping me focused and on track.

Special thanks to Matt Abar, Rabbi Alperowitz, Carol Alsman, Mark Bajakian, Dianna Cavalieri, Lynne Davies, Carol and Reggie Enos, Paul Fanizzi, Brad Fowler, David Gardner, Mark Leach, Joel Lehrer, Gayle Neckar, Rich Perozich, Anthony Smith and Martha Wadleigh.

Finally, I acknowledge Susan Driscoll and Kristin Oomen at iUniverse, Jennifer Fox and the entire marketing staff at American Airlines, who are truly special—both on the ground and in the air.

Bill Schneider
Provincetown, MA
January, 2007

About the Author

Brad Fowler, Song of Myself Photography

Bill Schneider is an accomplished freelance journalist, novelist, and screen-writer who enjoys traveling throughout the world. As a unique raconteur of love stories, Bill's characters are filled with dazzle, yet they emote tremendous intrigue and depth.

This is the third novel written by Bill and published under the ASJA Press banner of iUniverse. Bill's debut novel, *Second Chapter*, was published in April, 2005. A sequel, *Sand Dollar*, was published in July 2006.

When on solid ground, Bill resides in Provincetown, situated on the tip of Cape Cod, where he is surrounded by friends, pets and an extended family who enjoy the magnificent beauty of the national seashore. For more information, visit www.BillSchneider.us.

978-0-595-42748-2
0-595-42748-0

Printed in the United Kingdom
by Lightning Source UK Ltd.
136056UK00001B/420/A